MERCHANTS
OF VIRTUE

(Based on a true story)

Book One of
THE HUGUENOT CONNECTION
Trilogy

PAUL C.R. MONK

A BLOOMTREE PRESS book.

First published in 2016 by BLOOMTREE PRESS.

Copyright © Paul C. R. Monk 2016

ISBN 978-0-9934442-6-5

www.paulcrmonk.com

Cover design by David Ter-Avanesyan

BY THE SAME AUTHOR

In The Huguenot Connection trilogy:

Merchants of Virtue

Voyage of Malice

Land of Hope

Also in the Huguenot series:

Before The Storm 1685

May Stuart

Other works:

Strange Metamorphosis

Subterranean Peril

The death of Charles II in February 1685 enabled the Duke of York to accede to the throne as a Roman Catholic king. He became James II of England and Ireland, and James VII of Scotland.

The Duke's friend and cousin, Louis XIV of France, welcomed the news. It encouraged the French king to hasten his plans to complete the purge of non-Catholic subjects from his court, kingdom, and colonies, especially the Protestants, known in France as Huguenots.

These Huguenots had enjoyed freedom of worship, as well as political and civil rights guaranteed by the Edict of Nantes, which had been signed eighty-seven years earlier by Louis XIV's grandfather. Louis's plan to revoke the edict would consolidate France under one faith, one law, and one king.

Indeed, slowly but surely, Louis had already stripped the heretics of civil rights, ordered the destruction of their temples and schools, and restricted their fields of professional activity.

While James embarked on his Catholic kingship, Louis and his entourage perfected plans for the last push to persuade resisting Protestants to reconvert to the true religion. The final dragonnades were soon to be put into action.

1

19 August 1685

JEANNE DELPECH DE Castanet took a sip from the exquisite Chinese teacup. Suzanne was telling her about the arrival of Monsieur de Boufflers, which had been the talk of the town since yesterday.

'I wondered why there were so many carts travelling out from Montauban,' said Jeanne.

'Were there really?' said Suzanne with a hint of concern. Then, helping herself to another biscuit, with her usual merriment she said, 'These ones are flavoured with vanilla, you know.'

Jeanne could not help but notice that her sister had not only put on a little weight, she had aged slightly around the eyes. Jeanne wondered if she, too, would look the same in nine years' time, for that was how many years separated them.

Suzanne was past childbearing age already, which was not a bad thing. While Jeanne suffered her pregnancies with a certain facility, Suzanne had many times lost the baby before its term. But she was happy, and she had her 'miracle child,' as she called him. She had also married well, even though her husband, Robert Garrisson, was twenty-five years her senior. He was nonetheless good company, doted on his wife and son, and did not look at all his age.

'I was telling Robert only yesterday that it was high time I paid you a visit,' said Suzanne. 'Really, you ought to have stayed put, dear sister. And I am not so sure your husband will be happy about you returning.'

'Well, I am not happy about him leaving me on my own. His business concerns seem to be his only preoccupation of late. Wife and children in the country, and Monsieur can do as he pleases.'

'Worry not your pretty head, my dear. He has been meeting with Robert.'

'And that Maître Satur, I suspect, soliciting more money for his unscrupulous ventures, no doubt. Anyway, I am here now, and I am certainly not going all that way back, whether Monsieur de Boufflers chooses to stay or not.'

'Robert fears he has plans to stay,' said Suzanne, pouring out more tea. 'And now Robert wants me to leave. But if you are staying, then so shall I! Besides, I got a glimpse of Monsieur de Boufflers yesterday: he did not look at all like the person he is made out to be. In fact, he was all frills and colour, most becoming to the eye.'

'Clothes do not make the man, Suzanne!'

'Quite. And did you know, he even showed off his undergarment ruffles!' said Suzanne with a ring of laughter. 'I believe it is the fashion in Versailles. But tell me, my dear sister, what is the news from Verlhac?'

Jeanne related the recent tidings from the country: the children's playacting in the barn, the drought, the lengths to which farmers had to go to irrigate the land, the daily ritual of leading the cows to water, and the proliferation of mosquitoes after the recent storm.

Two pots of tea later, Suzanne showed Jeanne down the flagstone steps to the carriage entrance where a sedan chair was waiting. A bearer stood at either end.

'Really, my sister, I can walk.'

'You know what they say: by mid-August, the hazelnut has a full belly!' Suzanne had a way with words, and would always make them sound like they were chiming inside her. 'Now, in you get. And send for me as soon as the pangs begin.'

'I cannot sit in that box.'

'Well, you must. You are in no condition to cross the filthy streets in this heat. You might slip over. I shall not be responsible for a tragedy! In you go. You, your hazelnut, and all,' said Madame Garrisson.

Ever since Jeanne could remember, Suzanne won her way in the most mirthful fashion, and always attracted a smile. Jeanne, on the other hand, most often displayed a little thought-pleat across her brow.

'All right, if you want me to feel like Madame de Maintenon. But I shall send it back so that you can visit when the time comes.'

'I will, dear sister. I am in haste to meet little Pierre's new cousin!'

No sooner had Jeanne Delpech sat on the chair than the bearers lifted the poles, and the valet opened the smaller of the front doors. Amid amused rings of laughter from the ladies, the bearers stepped through the door into the sunny street. Then they marched westward across town.

'Take the market route, would you? I would like to call

at Monsieur Picquos's,' said Madame Delpech, feeling very much like a Parisian marquise.

*

With a flourish of his lace-cuffed hand the Marquis de Boufflers put the question of conversion to the intendant of Montauban, Urbain Le Goux de La Berchère.

'Swearing allegiance to the king is not enough,' said de Boufflers. 'The king's policy of one faith and one law must be enforced throughout the entire kingdom! There can be no more exceptions. We need to make this town entirely Catholic. However, it would be most disagreeable to our divine sovereign if we had to resort to the arrest and castigation of his own subjects. But can we avoid it? I have heard Montauban will be the hardest nut to crack.'

They were sitting in the sumptuous oak-panelled chamber of the town hall. Intendant de la Berchère sat back in his barley twist chair behind his walnut desk, arching together his lean fingers. Within the short time since he had taken up office in Montauban, he had come to know what made people here tick.

He said: 'The Huguenots preach about the individual's right to decide matters of spirituality, my Lord, but they are in truth like all bourgeois. They aspire to pre-eminence and a title. And they will stand in one block behind their prominent members whom they will follow like sheep.'

'Ah. So if we win over the Huguenot leaders we win the whole town,' said the marquis with false candour. As commander of the Sun King's dragoons he had to find out to what extent he could count on the intendant's complicity. And in fact, de la Berchère was turning out to be sharper and more sophisticated than his solemn and somewhat stoic appearance would have one believe, much more to the marquis' liking than Dubois, the previous administrator.

'Undoubtedly, my Lord, if not the whole *généralité*.' With a wry smile, de la Berchère reached over and served his illustrious visitor some more of his best Fronton wine.

The Marquis de Boufflers said: 'Then our first task, before we put forth our propositions, will be to acquire some substance for negotiation.'

'Indeed, my Lord,' said the intendant. And to show he not only grasped but also subscribed to the marquis' allusion to a dragonnade, he added: 'It will be wise to first remind them that their soft hands and soft bellies will not help them if their heads are too hard!'

'I could not have put it better myself,' said de Boufflers. 'Your name will go down in history, Sir, as the one who saved a multitude from torment and brought the fold back from the precipice of spiritual ruin.'

'I only seek to avoid unnecessary strife, my Lord, and desire what sits well with our good king . . .'

'Quite,' said de Boufflers, thoroughly satisfied, and he raised his glass. 'To king and country!'

'To king and country . . . and God!'

*

The pretty backdrop of peachy brick walls appeased Jeanne Delpech, and reassured her of her decision to return to Montauban. This was her home, the provincial town she so loved. Even animal muck and litter from the recent Catholic procession did not put her out. She was so looking forward to the year's gatherings.

Elizabeth would be eleven this year, Lulu was coming up for three, and little Paul was seven. He had clearly manifested a penchant for structure and order by his observances of God's tiny creatures that he pinned into his collection. She hoped her mother-in-law would not interfere too much in his upbringing. She hoped too that the Lord would help the king see clearly how the divine design did not advocate idolatry and forced ceremony, but freedom of thought and worship. However, for the time being, she banished such shadows from her brow.

Her bearers came to a halt under the brick arcades of the royal square peopled with shoppers, and then lowered her chair to the ground. She got out and ambled into the spacious, vaulted boutique, its deep shelves packed with rolls of colourful fabric and swathes of drapery.

She had known Monsieur Picquos since her late father arranged financing for him to purchase his boutique. He sold the finest textiles in the generality. But she had not stopped by for cloth. She had dropped in for a rare and expensive edible indulgence that came from Guadeloupe, where he possessed interests in a plantation. She had come to purchase some chocolate, a treat for Jacob, her husband, to sweeten the taste of her defiance.

'Madame Delpech,' said the draper with a bow after leaving a customer in the hands of his assistant.

Monsieur Picquos was a co-religionist who had suffered from the restrictions imposed by Louis XIV and his advisers—even if retail was the least affected of occupations, given its direct impact on the royal treasury. Monsieur Picquos, like most Huguenots, had learnt to battle on in the hope that the storm would pass and things would become re-established according to the Edict of Nantes.

'How nice to see you looking so well,' Monsieur Picquos continued.

Being in the country for so long had made her quite disregard her physical metamorphosis. It suddenly occurred to her how enormous she must look. But any embarrassment was quelled by experience—this was not her first pregnancy.

She gave him her thanks with a polite smile, and, glancing around, she was reassured to find the shop surprisingly quiet. But it was Sunday, a day when Huguenots, like Catholics, would normally be in church, if it were not for the fact that their Protestant temples had been demolished.

'When is the happy event due?'

'As soon as possible, I hope,' said Jeanne, fanning herself.

'You won't be leaving town, then.' Monsieur Picquos lowered his voice. 'Many say they are, because of de Boufflers. I have sent my wife and children to my cousin's, you know.'

'Oh? But do you really think such a man can cause a whole town to convert in one fell swoop? Just like that, on a whim?' said Jeanne, half in jest.

The draper looked blankly back at her.

*

Jacob Delpech de Castanet looked out into the street from the bourgeois comfort and coolness of his ground-floor study. He was standing in his tall townhouse in Rue de la Serre. The thick wooden shutters had been left ajar; the windows were closed. Distant church bells announced a quarter to noon as behind him the discussion continued.

'We are condemned, I am telling you,' said Maître Pierre Satur, a stout man in his early fifties.

'The king's intention is to eradicate all forms of religion, except Catholicism, naturally,' added Robert Garrisson, Jacob's friend and brother-in-law. Messieurs Satur and Garrisson were court attorneys and former members of the now banned Huguenot consistory.

Turning to face the room, Jacob said, 'That would constitute a grave transgression of the law. Would our king be unlawful? Why, article seven of the Edict of Nantes stipulates, does it not, that it is—'

Maître Satur held up his hand, and in the cavernous voice usually reserved for the courtroom, he said, 'It is permitted to all lords, gentlemen, and other persons making profession of the said religion called Reformed, to exercise the said religion in their houses . . .' Satur lowered his hand and continued in a more conversational tone of voice. 'I know it, we all know it by heart, my dear Monsieur Delpech. However, it does not alter the fact that he wants every one of his subjects to convert.'

Robert, who had been seated, stood up with surprising energy for his age, unfurling his lean, tall person made taller by his periwig and heels. 'Then, tell me, gentlemen,' he said, 'would you leave or abjure?'

Maître Pierre Satur tilted his head from side to side as if weighing up the odds, which made his periwig wobble. Then he took a sip from his goblet of Armagnac.

'For my part,' said Jacob, 'forsaking my faith is beyond me. I would rather leave for pastures new if I could.'

'Indeed, many are preferring exile,' said Robert.

Jacob continued, 'But, I cannot. I have my properties and

my land. Not to mention my dear wife, who is on the verge of her labours, and who is justifiably against the idea anyway. Our roots are in this soil.'

Maître Satur said, 'Moreover, it will soon be impossible to leave the town, let alone traverse the frontier. Get caught leaving the country nowadays, and it's off to the galleys!' Then, in a graver tone, he announced, 'Boufflers has declared that his men-at-arms are at but a day's march. And when they get here, they are to be billeted in Huguenot homes.'

'Outrageous, surely not!' said Jacob.

'You have read the reports from Bearn, have you not?' said Maître Satur.

'Yes, yes. I find it hard to believe, though.'

'And the dragonnades of sixty-one, you believe those, do you not?'

'Yes, but . . .'

'They will be here tomorrow, Jacob,' said Robert solemnly.

With determination, Jacob declared, 'We are by far the majority here. We shall just have to stand together.'

Jacob's guests did not react with the same vigour. Instead, lowering his voice, Robert said, 'And what of our mutual investment? Any news?'

'None, I fear,' said Satur. 'But remember, gentlemen, the higher the stakes, the greater the risk . . .'

'But you are the one who advised us to pay into it, Maître,' said Jacob.

'And I stand to lose a good deal more than anyone.'

Jacob was about to respond when footsteps compelled him to glance out onto the street. He caught sight of two bearers sweating under their felt hats, and between them a sedan chair with the curtains drawn back. His heart quickened with both discontent and contentment now that, along with his children whom he had greeted at home earlier, he once again had a full house.

'It is Jeanne,' he said. 'She need know nothing of this; I do not want to worry her in her condition.' Jacob rang the little brass bell on his desk and called out to Anette, the maid.

Turning back to his visitors with renewed optimism, he said, 'But come, gentlemen, the heat has abated, this year's yield promises to be excellent, we have bread and wine, and we have our faith. Will you do me the honour of joining us for our midday repast?'

*

After evening prayer, Elizabeth, Paul, and Louise Delpech kissed their parents goodnight.

They were sleeping when, two hours later, Jacob looked in on each of them, holding his chamberstick. Sensing his father's presence, Paul awoke. Jacob put down the bronze candleholder, sat on the boy's bed, and held him to his bosom for a full minute.

What was to become of him and his sisters in this world gone mad? Should he take them and their mother away to a safer country? But how would they cope with a different language? How would they fit into a new culture? Or ought he to remain and pray to God that the winds of folly would soon blow over? What if the king died? What if the future belonged to those who waited patiently? He laid the boy back down onto his bed, and covered him up with just a sheet of linen that smelt of lavender.

The seven-year-old turned over. Contented, he slipped back into sleep.

By the time Jacob entered his bedroom, Jeanne was lying in bed, propped up on pillows, with the shutter half-open for air, and a window gauze inserted into the frame to keep out the mosquitoes. Her candelabra flickered beside her on the wooden marriage chest. Jacob stepped round the rocking cot made ready for the new baby, put down his chamberstick on the washstand, and then sat down on the edge of the high bed, placing a heavy hand on the carved wooden post. Heartened though he was to see his wife and children, their presence did not take away any of his anxiety—quite the contrary.

Jeanne knew better than anyone in the world when her husband had doubts. She had seen it when he had been obliged to sell his practice, when he had ventured into a new occupation, when their second daughter was called to heaven after a short illness at the age of five. She placed her hand on his temple and brushed back his hair over his ear.

The young lady he had married twelve years earlier had grown to love him. Her devotion shone through in the way she had made his house their home. It shone through when he saw their children.

Turning to her, he grasped her hand to arrest its caress, and said, 'Jeanne, you really ought not to have travelled in your condition.'

'I told you, Jacob, I want the baby to be born in Montauban, like our other children.' She tugged her hand free, ran it down his arm, and slipped it around his wrist. 'I am the one who is carrying it.'

There was no rational case against that. He would have to try to force his wishes upon her.

'I am not going to argue with you, Jeanne. My decision is final.'

She let his hand drop onto the bed, and said, 'I am not one of your farmhands, Jacob . . . I suspect you want me out of the way so that you can put together another moneymaking venture with your lawyer friend.'

'No, it is not that. I told you, there is little risk there. And besides, Maître Satur takes care of everything: he is the one in relation with the shipowners.'

'But doesn't the Bible say it is wrong to lend money for money's sake? And you know what my father used to say, that money put into New World ventures is more often than not employed to purchase slaves.'

'Jeanne, I would do no such thing.'

'I know you would not, Jacob, but I am not so sure about Maître Satur.'

'Well, if it will reassure you, I am not planning another moneymaking venture, as you call it. I shall have enough on my plate with the harvest.' He took her hand in both of his, and softening his tone, he pleaded, 'Please, Jeanne, you must leave first thing tomorrow morning with the children.'

'I cannot . . .'

'My dear Jeanne, listen. I . . . I fear the immediate future does not bode well.'

Jeanne sat immobile as she studied the gravity of her husband's expression. 'Monsieur Picquos was not exaggerating when he told me the soldiers are coming then.'

'I fear not.'

Taking hold of his right hand again, she said, 'All the

more reason to stay together, Jacob, as we always have. We are a family, are we not?' She pressed his hand against the tight mound of her belly, and she said, 'Come, let us pray.'

2

20 August 1685

AN HOUR AFTER sunrise, two raps of the doorknocker made Jacob and Jeanne look up from their draught of chocolate.

Jeanne, holding her belly with one hand, pushed back her chair, then made her way from the panelled dining room to the spacious vestibule. She began to climb the wide darkwood staircase to the upper rooms where her children still lay sleeping.

Jacob had hurried to the window in the adjoining study that looked onto the street. He now peered between the wooden shutters that had been pulled ajar to screen the room from the day's heat. The maid, with fear in her eyes, had moved into the vestibule and now stood at the front door, waiting for the signal.

'It is one of Robert's servants,' said Jacob with a sigh of relief. 'Open the door, Anette, and let him in.'

It was that time of day when a large number of chamber pots were emptied out of upper-floor windows and, in his precipitation, the lackey had trodden on a turd. He was scraping his shoe on the wrought-iron boot scraper when the massive green door opened. He stepped inside the entrance hall which led to the study, the rear corridor, and the staircase. Inside the door stood a wooden bench where people could remove their street footwear and garments, but the lackey remained standing.

'Speak up, my boy,' said Jacob from the study doorway.

'Monsieur, my master has sent me to tell you that soldiers are entering through Moustier gate. They are in great numbers, some on foot, some on horseback. Even greater numbers, some say thousands, are entering through the gate of Villebourbon.'

Despite her imminent labour, Jeanne, who had paused on the intermediate landing, hurried up the stairs. She was normally of a calm and rational disposition and not subject to panic; however, these days, it was every Huguenot mother's fear that her children would be taken away from her. She knew how easy it was for powerful men to amend and interpret the law as it suited them. When Madame Larieux's husband died, the authorities took the opportunity of her mourning to assign her three daughters to a convent, so that they could be brought up in the religion of the state, according to a new law.

Jacob sent word to his own lackey to forewarn his mother and widowed sister, who resided in the west part of town, a stone's throw away from the recently demolished temple. In this way, word spread from family to family, and in its wake marched de Boufflers's army, an army made up for the most part of Swiss and German mercenaries.

*

The bells of Saint Jacques chimed the hour. Today might be the day the Huguenot safe haven would become Catholic again, thought intendant de la Berchère. It gave him a real sense of virtue and piety to win over the heretics and rid the generality of heresy, for the sake of national unity, once and for all.

Unfurling a scroll that lay on his desk, he turned his head to the Marquis de Boufflers, who was standing at his side with the Bishop of Montauban.

The intendant said: 'In accordance with your instructions, my Lord Marquis, with Monseigneur Jean-Baptiste-Michel, we have drawn up a list of Protestant homes to be billeted, here.' His forefinger ran down a long list of names. 'Along with the number of troopers they are to accommodate.'

The Right Reverend Bishop Jean-Baptiste-Michel Colbert, a large-shouldered and pot-bellied man in his mid-forties, gave a little cough. And in his beautiful tenor voice, he said: 'The numbers have been carefully pondered, my Lord, in relation to the type of house and the, shall we say, potential resistance that is likely to be encountered.'

'Excellent, Your Grace,' said the marquis, who proceeded in opening a leather pouch he was holding. While pulling out bundles of printed billets, he continued: 'All you do now is write the name of the owner on a billet with the corresponding number of soldiers, and sign it.' The last wad of printed billets fell onto the desk. 'The simplest plans often make for the most effective results,' he said with a flourish of the wrist.

The billets were filled out, signed, then passed on to the commanding officers of small sections of troops. This took some time, and it was not until past lunchtime that many sections were informed of their quarters which they then had to locate.

*

After taking note of his billet, Lieutenant Didier Ducamp glanced at the sun from the northern double-vaulted arcade of the main square, where he and his men—four Germans, two French, two Swiss—had settled after the march into town. He cast his eyes to his left towards a cobbled lane. 'Right, men, Rue de la Serre is that way, I wager. We'll be needing a townsman to guide us, preferably a Catholic,' he said in his dry humour, as much to himself as to his men, half of whom could barely understand him anyway.

In truth, though, the lieutenant really did not care what religion his guide belonged to, so long as he led them to their destination. He knew from experience that every man was made of the same stuff inside; he had seen men of every religion slaughtered on the battlefield. They all spilled their guts the same when their bellies were sliced. They all bled red blood, and shat through their arses in a like manner. Besides, he was beginning to dislike this dragonnade business. It had been amusing in Pau at first, traipsing through bourgeois' homes, but now it was becoming tedious. It was not what the army was made for. That said, duty was duty, and in another three years, he might even retire with enough money to get a tavern and a new wife.

There happened to be a crowd of onlookers on the corner. They had stopped to witness the scene of a Huguenot grandee flapping around at his townhouse, where soldiers were piling in through the large carriage door.

'You there,' called the lieutenant, designating a bourgeois who looked like he was enjoying the show. Ducamp, who was over six feet tall, strode the few yards that separated them. He had to raise his voice above the ambient din of bawled commands, Germanic grunts, marching boots, the clank of steel, and horses stamping and snorting. He said: 'Do you know Rue de la Serre? I'm looking for a tall house with a large green door. Belongs to a certain Jacob Delpech.'

'I do indeed, Sir,' said the bourgeois, proud to be of service. He took a few strides away from the din and said: 'It so happens I live opposite. It is a spacious townhouse. Monsieur Delpech is of a long line of nobles of the robe, you know, except for his father, who was a physician, I believe. I am sure you will find all the comforts you require there.'

Ducamp liked jurists' homes: they were well-organised, and most of them were well-stocked. Things were picking up. He was looking forward to a decent night's kip in a good bed. And he wondered if his new host had any worthy maids, or daughters.

'If you would be so kind as to show us the way there, we shall find comfort all the sooner, shall we not?' said Ducamp as a quip, though the humour in his voice was hardly perceptible.

Over the next few hours, the clamour of four thousand men of war gradually spread out in small sections like Ducamp's from the epicentre of the town. Some lanes were made of dark-grey pebbles shaped like pork kidneys that marchers cursed; others were hard-earth thoroughfares made dusty in the high-noon sun.

*

The sickening ruckus of hobnailed boots on cobbles grew louder in Rue de la Serre, as the banging of iron knockers on doors proliferated. Inside the tall house with the green door, Jacob, Jeanne, and their three children came to the last verse of a favourite psalm as the doorknocker rapped with authority.

The song always helped Jacob Delpech fight panic in times of uncertainty. And he must remain in charge of his emotions. He was, after all, responsible for the safety and well-being of his family and household. And he could not deny they were all probably about to suffer, unless he put his faith to one side.

Jeanne sensed his inner turmoil. She pressed his forearm with silent and soulful determination, as on other occasions during their married life. But they were ready to confront the soldiers, even though they had both secretly hoped their house would be passed over, given Jacob's status.

He was a landowner and wealthy merchant now, had been so since the decree five years earlier that had forced Huguenot notaries to either sell their practices or abjure. His organisational skills had served him well in managing his farms and selling their produce of fruit, cattle, and cereal. He was one of the first to plant maize, the versatile crop from the New World, in the great fertile plain that surrounded the town. He had also become quite a botanist, and studied water usage and plant requirements for more efficient growth. This resulted in recent yields being consistently higher than average, and his conversion from records of law to record yields had not transpired without some envy.

God had come to try them before; if it pleased Him to try them again, then so be it, Jeanne had told him. They would face up to this hurdle in the same way that they had confronted Jacob's professional reconversion, with unwavering resolve but without straying from the road of God's love and ultimate reward.

She ushered the children up the stairs to their first-floor rooms. That was the plan.

The doorknocker hammered again.

'King's men, open the door!' hurled a soldier's voice.

Jacob gave the nod to Anette to open up as he joined her in the vestibule, where she stood at the front door, speechless and mouse-like.

'This the house of Jacob Delpech?' said the tall, rugged figure that dwarfed her, even though she was standing two steps higher.

'Yes, Sir, I am he,' said Jacob, stepping into view. 'Who do I have the pleasure of . . .'

Lieutenant Ducamp had no time for bourgeois talk. He had a job to do. He held out his billet and read. 'Conforming with the law, Monsieur Jacob Delpech shall give quarter to nine soldiers and will give to these soldiers light, board, and lodging.'

In times of conflict, soldiers were lodged with the lower classes for a specified number of days.

'You must be mistaken,' said Jacob, feigning not to understand what was happening. 'I am Jacob Delpech de Castanet.'

'Read for yourself, Jacob Delpech de Castanet!' growled the lieutenant, holding up the billet in Jacob's face.

Didier Ducamp had seen the same mock incomprehension before in Bearn. It was becoming a bore. Did the bourgeois really think they were dealing with morons? He had to admit, though, he had fallen for the comedy the first couple of times. On those occasions, he had marched back to his commanding officer to check his information. However, now with experience, not to mention a right rollicking from his commander, he had learnt to disregard any theatricality and get on with the mission at hand.

When he thought about it now, it made him laugh to think that he, who feared neither God nor the devil, had become a better missionary than the Bishop of Bearn.

He pushed his way into the premises. His men followed suit without a thought for the boot scraper, and soon smells of sweat, oil, powder, leather, and horse shit filled the largest reception room of the house.

It was always an eye-opener to see how the upper crust lived. Useless ornaments on carved and embroidered furniture, paintings and tapestries on walls, and books, rows of them, all leather-bound, always a good sign of prosperity. Oh yes, money had left its mark here. It was a reassuring thought because he and his men could eat a stableful of horses. This, he sensed, would be better than the last billet in Pau which was barren as an old hen. And it had turned out messy too.

The slip of a hand had accidentally popped the proprietor's neck while they were helping him drink a 'restorative' to give him courage to abjure. Of course, the lieutenant had learnt since that you had to be extra careful how you handled penpushers, who were soft as young pigeons.

As the eight mercenaries in the pay of the king traipsed into the room, Didier Ducamp turned to his second in command, and gave him a hardly perceptible nod of appreciation. It meant there was no point in rushing this one, at least not while the storehouse was full and their bellies empty.

'Bring us bread, meat, cheese, and wine,' said Lieutenant Ducamp.

'Listen here, Sir, you really ought to check with the intendant. I am a gentleman—'

'And we are the king's men!' said Ducamp. 'And hungry men with it. Now, do you love and respect your king?'

'I do.'

'Do you respect the law of this land?'

'Yes, Sir.'

'Then fetch us our grub and grog, unless you prefer we help ourselves.'

Jacob could but agree to do as was required of him.

'We'll find our quarters ourselves,' said Ducamp.

The next moment, the wooden staircase was trembling under the footfalls of nine massive men-at-arms. Jeanne was on her way down, with her children in tow, having considered it would be better to keep them with her.

'Gentlemen,' she said boldly and with an empathetic smile. She managed not to let the organic stench of manure and body fluids overpower her nerve. 'We have prepared a large room for you on the second floor, where you will be comfortable, I am sure.'

The soldiers laughed out loud and barged past her without a thought for her condition. Indeed, it was fortunate she was standing, with her children filed behind her like goslings, on the wide intermediate landing. Otherwise, she may well have been flattened against the wall.

'My mother is with baby, Sirs, please have some respect!' said a determined little voice. It belonged to Paul, Jeanne's son of seven.

A soldier leered back over the banister with an amused jeer. But he was not staring at the boy. He was looking at his elder sister, Elizabeth. The soldier seemed to be sizing her up; then he looked away in exasperation.

'Bah, flat as a battledore!' he grumbled.

His marching partner behind him then quipped: 'Give it another six months. If it bleeds, it breeds; that's what my ol' man used to say.'

By now, Jacob was standing at the foot of the stairs. 'Gentlemen, I protest,' he said firmly. 'Not under my roof will thou speak foul.'

He took his wife's hand and led her down into the vestibule and into the dining room while the soldiers continued into the first-floor corridor.

The bedroom doors upstairs could be heard being rattled, and forced open one by one. This was invariably followed by the clang of metal landing on the floor, which was in turn followed by the creak of bed ropes.

The harassment, though not physical, had shattered Jacob's sense of justice. It harked back to the day when he was told he would have to give up his practice. Then, too, he had felt that his world was about to cave in. However, as then, he still had his faith, and the love of his wife. She placed a hand on his shoulder as they knelt down to pray.

*

A good thing his uninvited guests missed the scene, busy as they were with their installation upstairs.

Jacob had got to his feet by the time the soldiers reappeared. They were visibly satisfied with the self-attributed quarters and now were ready for food.

They had been marching from Bearn since Friday. Bakers, who had been commissioned to produce bread in abundance, had not been able to provide enough for four thousand extra mouths. And by the time Ducamp had entered the town, albeit early in the morning, there was not a quignon of bread to be found. Was this the way to treat men who risked their lives in war? They had finished their own provisions of dried sausage and were now so ravenous they would put raw flesh between their teeth.

On seeing nothing served, panic, a sense of injustice, and then the fire of wrath consumed the pits of their bellies, where only hunger had previously growled. One soldier grabbed Jacob by the lapels, slammed him against the panelling. The thick-set man brought Jacob's face level with his own, and, in a Germanic accent, he bellowed: 'Food, where's the bloody food! You want me ask your fat wench?'

'Easy, Willheim, man!' said Ducamp with the stamp of authority. 'Remember what happened last time.'

Between gritted teeth, the dragoon growled something in German, and let Jacob drop to the floor. A second later, Monique, the old cook, thankfully shuffled in with a leg of ham, bread, cheese, a wicker-covered jug of wine, and pewter tankards. Ducamp's soldiers lunged for the table with their knives and sat down astride the benches.

'Thank you,' said Jacob, wiping the soldier's saliva from his face.

Didier Ducamp stood tall and stoic, in spite of the scare that reminded him he was responsible for containing these savages and would have to be vigilant at all times. He said to Jacob: 'If you want us out of here, you know what to do. Abjure, man!'

3

21 August 1685

UNDER THE EDICT of Nantes which ended the wars of religion in France, Protestants had been granted safe havens in the form of towns in which they could freely practice their faith.

However, Louis XIV craved to unify his kingdom under one religion, which meant stamping out reformist hotbeds. Slowly at first, but surely, Protestant rights were ground down, protective city walls were destroyed, temples and schools were demolished, and government and judicial offices became restricted to Catholics only.

The most versatile among the Huguenot population of Montauban seeking employment in a royal office became Catholic. Nonetheless, despite the discrimination and the influx of Catholic clerks and suchlike, Montauban families had remained largely Protestant, especially those who wanted to get on in business.

So all about the town, thousands of well-to-do families were undergoing a similar degree of intimidation and ill treatment. It seemed to them, as it did to Jacob, that the very men paid through their taxes to protect them were treating the town like a vanquished enemy city, and were bent on destroying its very fabric with no respect for its past.

Most of these troopers were in fact mercenaries of Germanic stock. They cared little for the tradition and culture of the French generality, which made them ideal candidates for the job. They had no emotional ties; all they wanted was to earn money to send back to their homeland, or to squander as they saw fit.

Gentlemen's homes became crowded with belching, farting, snoring men whose libido was quickened by the southern skies. The most audacious invariably grabbed inside their breeches whenever a lady of the house passed by.

*

Jacob looked as though he had aged ten years in a single night, harassed as he was by the demands of nine ruffians.

He had insisted on waiting on them himself to save his household any further humiliation and to keep the soldiers from temptation. Besides, he would not have slept anyway, what with his harvest plans in turmoil—and no news from Maître Satur of their latest venture. At least he had managed to negotiate with the lieutenant to take repossession of his bedroom so that his wife and children could rest. In return, he agreed to generously provide the men with as much food and wine as they could put down their gullets. A costly compromise for sure, but it meant the soldiers slept the afternoon away in a drunken torpor, which enabled Jacob and his family to regroup and reinforce their unity and conviction through prayer.

On this same day, the intendant sent out a party of conciliatory officers to heretics' homes. It was crucial for him to strike while the iron was hot to win the town back over to

Roman Catholicism, and to avoid as many 'spillages' as possible.

Bertrand Nolen—a well-mannered man with a white philosopher's beard, wearing a dark-leather doublet with a folded-down ruff from a previous decade—was one of these missionary officers. He had spent the morning pounding the cobblestones, trying to talk some sense into the Protestant patriarchs. He bore witness time and again to ransacked homes in complete disorder. The dishevelled Huguenots saw his coming as a link to the higher spheres that could perhaps put an end to their sufferance. Nine times out of ten, Bertrand Nolen had to first hear out their remonstrances, their rage, and the accusations of wrongdoing. Bertrand's strategy was to let them empty their bag of grievances so they would be in a better disposition to hear his arguments. Of course they were right: they were victims of higher affairs of state, out of his control. Of course they deserved compensation.

At present, he was standing, with his tall beaver hat under his arm and an abjuration certificate in his hand, in the entrance hall of the large house in Rue de la Serre. He had known Monsieur Delpech from when Jacob worked as a notary.

'It is up to you,' said Monsieur Nolen, brandishing the blank certificate. 'You can make it cease now, right this minute, with a simple signature. That is all it takes for you to recover your household, Sir. Not only that, but as a Catholic, you may take up your former profession, if you so wish. Our king only wants his kingdom to be united again, as it once was not so long ago. Is that so wrong?'

'You ask of me to betray my very soul,' said Jacob, palming

his straggling hair from his forehead. 'My innermost convictions which make me the man that I am, Sir.'

'Then if not for the sake of your livelihood, do it for the sake of your family. For is not vanity a sin? I believe your wife is soon to bear her child. Will she not fare better in a quiet room in a tranquil house?'

Jacob knew this argument had some substance, that he could be accused of taking his family hostage for his personal concerns. It even presented a respectable pretext for him to forsake his religion. But Jeanne, who had been standing by the stairs, raised her skirts slightly and stepped into the vestibule.

'No, Sir,' she said, to Monsieur Nolen's regret. 'I for one could never live with myself if we abjured our spiritual heritage, our simple and pure faith in God as our Saviour preached it, without artifice. It is what keeps us strong against adversity and injustice, Sir. It is the very fibre of our being. I would rather go without earthly possessions than be deprived of our Lord and His eternal promise.'

'You have my answer,' said Jacob, who felt the force of righteousness behind him again. 'We shall not abjure: we shall endure.'

'Then I am afraid endure you shall,' said Monsieur Nolen, placing his certificate with grave regret back into his leather shoulder pouch. 'You have been given the opportunity to save yourselves from the imminent storm. I have tried my best; our elite have tried and will continue to do so despite your obstinacy.' He turned and made for the door. 'But let me leave you in the hope that our conversation will stay with you, that you may see reason yet. May you know, Sir, Madame, that it will never be too late to abjure and bear allegiance to your king once again. May God be with you.'

Bertrand Nolen gave a prolonged bow, sweeping his tall hat before him. He knew his sincerity had at least touched their hearts, and he felt better in the knowledge that he had done all he could to bring these poor souls back into the fold. He stepped back into the street, positioned his hat on his head, and continued on his crusade.

4

23 August 1685

'MY LORDS, GENTLEMEN,' said intendant Le Goux de La Berchère, 'dare I say there has been some heated debate this afternoon.' He paused with the solemnity of one used to public speaking.

Intendant Le Goux de La Berchère was standing—immaculately attired in black breeches and stockings, a velvet doublet with white cuffs, and silver-buckle shoes that gave him extra poise— before an assembly of Huguenots in the large bureau in the town hall. The bishop was to his left, and on his right stood Louis Lefranc de Lacary, the president of the election bureau, who was indeed his right-hand man. Monsieur de Boufflers was absent. Impatient as he was to get the job done, he had taken a battalion of dragoons on a preliminary excursion to convert surrounding towns and villages from Albias to Realville and Caussade to Negrepelisse.

The intendant continued in his measured style. 'But we have made progress, gentlemen. Indeed, may I venture to say that we all agree that we are on the same side. We are all of Christian faith who believe in Jesus Christ, our Saviour. Are we not?'

The intendant again punctuated his irrefutable statement with a pause to take in the nods from the handpicked delegation. He had invited about thirty leading Huguenots—two aristocrats, eleven lawyers, seven bourgeois, and a handful of merchants—to a conciliatory debate at the town hall after lunch. This was always a good time to negotiate with the local population, so thought the intendant. However, today, despite the drowsy heat of the closed room and the organic mixture of sweat and fading perfume, his guests had kept up their guard with gravity. They demanded more time for deliberation, and to enlarge the assembly to embrace more of their fellow Huguenots.

De la Berchère knew they were now expecting a few words in his closing speech on the regiments of soldiers quartered throughout the town. However, he was not going to oblige. Instead, with a certain satisfaction, he said: 'I invite you all to examine your conscience, to weigh the reasons that have driven you from your natural church, the church of your king and country. I would like you to see if the minor differences proclaimed by a minority of reformists are truly worth the risk of losing your livelihood. I pray the night will bring good counsel, that tomorrow, we shall be united once again here for the common good. I propose we meet tomorrow morning at eight o'clock. That will be all.'

An instant of immobility fell upon the assembly. It was broken when, as the intendant turned to the bureau president to close the session, an incredulous voice rose up from the Huguenot ranks.

'But, my Lord, what of the soldiers in our homes?'

A rumble of 'hear hears' and shuffling feet on the polished parquet seconded Maître Pierre Satur's objection.

De la Berchère turned back to face the assembly, and in all simplicity, he said: 'As I stated earlier, let us hope we can reach a satisfactory conclusion tomorrow.'

'With all due respect, Your Honour,' said one merchant, standing a few yards to the side of Satur, 'my home is like a pigsty, and my poor wife is about to go into labour. The men go about the place with no regard whatsoever for her privacy. I found one of them urinating in a vase this morning. There was another, in full view in the dining room, trying to burst a boil on his posterior. I pray you make this cease, that common sense will prevail!'

'What is your name, Sir?' said de la Berchère above the mutterings of empathy and remonstration.

'Delpech, my Lord. Jacob Delpech.'

'Well, Monsieur Delpech, I unfortunately cannot vouch for every one of the four thousand men of arms billeted around town. And no doubt they lack your refinement.' He left a beat for the complaisant chuckling from his sympathisers, then continued, 'But they are warriors after all, battle-hardened through years of protecting the king's subjects from the enemy. However, our Most Reverend bishop here will, I am sure, be only too glad to offer you absolution, and your hardships will cease. It is as simple as that, Monsieur Delpech.'

The bishop stepped up to speak, his fine voice resounding high and sober above the remonstrations of the errant flock.

'Indeed, gentlemen, if you would rather rid your homes of the king's men today, you only need to come and see the intendant or myself directly after this meeting.'

Intendant de la Berchère then turned to the bureau

president, who closed the session. All in all, it had gone better than expected.

*

Urbain Le Goux de La Berchère found himself, if not alarmed, then surprised at his own lack of feeling towards the suffering of his fellow citizens.

Indeed, he would be the first to admit he would not make a very sympathetic Samaritan; he simply had neither the patience nor the disposition. However, as the assembly evacuated the bureau, he found comfort in the knowledge that every character type serves a purpose in God's design, and that he had been put on earth to administer, and there was nothing wrong in that. There had to be unemotional types; otherwise, who else would be able to make amends in a crisis?

He recalled once in his younger days seeing an old woman collapse in a Parisian thoroughfare after being brushed by his coach. Instead of advising his driver to find a physician, he had thought it more appropriate to summon a priest and an undertaker directly. Anyone with a clear head could see that the old lady's goose was cooked, for she did not look very well at all. A short time after the incident, he received a letter from the woman's son, who thanked him for his presence of mind and for not incurring unnecessary expense for the family. Thanks to the then-young Urbain's detached demeanour, the old lady was saved from being laid to rest in the communal grave due to lack of coinage.

The whole incident had since given Urbain Le Goux de La Berchère the courage to be his natural self. After all, was it not thanks to people of his fibre that humanity had been able to forge ahead in the face of adversity? Such was the tenor of his thoughts when, as the last of the Huguenots evacuated the room, he turned to the bishop and said, 'How much longer, do you think?'

'Not long now, I hope, my Lord,' said Bishop Jean-Baptiste-Michel, as genuinely concerned as a father waiting for his newborn baby. 'Deep down, they are all desperate to convert, but no one dares take the first step.'

The intendant said, 'The fact is they have been living in denial. They know how much easier life would be if they embraced the will of our king.'

'I pray the night will draw out their inhibitions,' said the bishop.

'Well put,' said the intendant. 'I dare say another night with the soldiers will work wonders.'

Then, turning to Lefranc de Lacary, the bureau president, he said, 'However, it might be a good idea to send an agent to Monsieur Satur's house, to reiterate our proposition and comfort him that the others are simply waiting to follow his lead.'

'As you wish, my Lord,' said Lefranc with a bow.

'Moreover,' continued de la Berchère, glancing at the bishop, 'to save time in the long run, it may well be worthwhile to set up a budget for the most prominent conversions.'

The bishop said, 'A small price to pay to bring back the lost sheep into the fold.'

He was determined to embrace the wayward lambs with dignity and pardon, and lead them on dutifully as their spiritual father should. Abjuration certificates were indeed at that very moment being pressed in their thousands. With secret excitement, the bishop took his leave to continue preparations for the imminent absolutions of the multitude.

*

Lieutenant Ducamp had fallen asleep on the comfortable divan in the study. He dreamt of fields, sun, war, and of a frayed black cloak gradually falling over him, slowly blotting out the living light. This was the succession of visions that often came to haunt his dreams. Was the cloak the shadow of death? Did it mean he was struck off God's list and would fall into nothingness?

He awoke.

A distinct smell filled his nostrils, and in his confusion, he sat bolt upright, searching his body in case he was on fire. Still groggy-headed from drink and dejected by his dream, he scanned the floor near an empty bottle of red wine. Beside it, a half-smoked cigar roll had burnt itself out, leaving a black burn mark on the waxed parquet. Yet, the distinct smell was still very present and getting stronger. It was the smell of war.

Most of his men were lying around like barrels over the floor, snoring from excess booze. The lieutenant quickly pulled on his boots. He sniffed around the fireplace that had not been used since April, then climbed the stairway three steps at a time.

At the same time, Jeanne Delpech, who had finally dozed after a sleepless night, awoke in her bedroom with a feeling of insecurity, a feeling worsened by concerns for the harvest at Verlhac. Had she known about the dragonnade, she would have stayed behind; indeed, she would have left the realm as her husband had once suggested. But such worries

35

were wiped away when she saw that two of her children were missing.

A knocking and rolling sound, accompanied by a burning smell, seemed to be coming from the room across the corridor where her son, Paul, normally slept. She pushed herself up from the bed, and, holding her bump, she hurried across the room.

She opened her door and stepped into the corridor just as Lieutenant Ducamp appeared at the top of the stairs, a dozen yards to her right. He stopped and stared at her as she swept across to the opposite room.

She burst in. Her son was squatting in front of the chimney, where a soldier was pouring liquid lead into a mould to make musket balls. The boy held a clutch of them. The place looked like an army camp with a bedroll half-unfurled on the floor and the contents of a knapsack scattered all around. A tinderbox, flint and steel, and a tin cup, spoon, and bowl lay around the hearth. In the fire, the remains of the legs of a chair had burned into embers.

'Come here, Paul!' she said, firmly but not in anger. She seized the boy, who rolled the lead balls into the green dragoon bonnet lying on the floor, and she pulled him out of the room.

Lieutenant Ducamp no longer focused on the familiar smell. Instead, his attention turned to two voices counting alternately in German in the bedroom in front of him: '*Funf, funf, sechs, sechs, sieben, sieben, acht, acht, nein, nein.*' One was the deep voice of a soldier, the other that of a child.

Ducamp opened the door and found the girl in her room, bouncing on a German trooper's knee. The soldier stopped. He looked frankly at the lieutenant, then back to the girl with a smile. He stroked her fair head and let her slide off his knee. Ducamp snatched her by the hand, which made her squeal. He pulled her out of the room, then dragged her the length of the corridor to where her distraught-looking mother was standing with her son.

'For Christ's sake, keep 'em out of sight!'

*

Jeanne sat upon the four-poster, her back cushioned with a bolster against the carved wooden headboard, and her two eldest children nestled around her. Lulu was asleep in the rocking cot which was almost too small for her now. It had been brought down from the storage room for her new brother or sister.

'But he said he had a daughter my age,' said Elizabeth, with her head on her mother's lap. 'He said she was pretty just like me.'

'Do as I tell you, children. Never leave my sight. You must promise to God.'

'Yes, Mother, we promise,' said Paul.

'Why is the French soldier so nasty to us?' said Elizabeth.

'He is not,' said Jeanne, realising that he had probably saved her child from a calamity. 'Now sing with me, children, quietly.'

The children joined her as she softly sang, 'Call upon me in the day of trouble. I will deliver thee . . .'

Hurried footsteps on the stairs interrupted their psalm. Jeanne anxiously listened to the sound of someone pacing up the corridor. Her face expressed relief when her husband burst into the room.

After a pause to take in the scene of his family huddled

together, he said, 'The delegation stood firm.'

'Thank goodness,' said Jeanne.

By force of habit, he strode over to the cot, placed between the bed and the tall wardrobe with carved lozenge panels, where Louise was still sleeping. Then he continued in a more controlled voice, 'Only one abjured. Tomorrow's meeting at eight o'clock is open to more of us.'

'How much longer must we endure?' said Jeanne in a lower voice. 'I long to bathe, or at least—'

At that instant, the bedroom door was thrust open, and the soldier from Paul's room opposite looked inside. He said in his thick Germanic accent: 'Abjure, and we leave you in peace!' Then he withdrew and marched off down the corridor, and down the stairs. This was nothing new: soldiers kept bursting in with the same message.

'They will not let us rest,' said Jeanne. 'I dare not even change—'

Before Jacob could answer, there came the ringing of a brass bell from downstairs. Moving to the door, he said, 'I hope that with more of us present tomorrow, we can persuade them that we stand as one, and that will be enough to discourage them in their villainy, and give them every reason to leave us in peace. Bear up a little longer, my dear wife. United, we will stand strong.'

The bell rang again, this time with more urgency. In a perpetual bid to keep his family out of harm's reach, Jacob hurried back downstairs.

5

24 August 1685

DUCAMP'S SOLDIERS KEPT Jacob up most of the night.

He was a walking wreck when, the next morning, he made his way to the town hall, as did one hundred and seventy-nine other co-religionists. Yet he looked forward to this meeting more than any other he could remember in the annals of Montauban. He was confident it would allow the Protestant city to affirm its identity. He looked forward to getting on with his harvest preparations which he cherished more than ever, as he did having his family around him in the gathering season. He regretted quarrelling with Jeanne over Maître Satur.

How right she had been to warn him against making money for money's sake. It would have been more Christianly to use it to work new land, and to employ more people. Lending money, as Calvin stated, was a fine mechanism when put to the good of others, but was plain usury when it was for pure personal profit. And to think he had knowingly turned a blind eye as to its application in Satur's shipping ventures. He had not wanted to know the details because he knew deep inside that it could well be used to finance not only the purchase and transport of New World produce to Europe, but the transport of slaves to America. For he well knew that a cargo ship could not leave for the Americas with an empty hold. He decided he would pull out of Satur's moneylending schemes and New World ventures.

Presided over by Lefranc, the debate centred on why the people of Montauban had slipped away from the religion of their ancestors. Were their differences not merely the relic of religious upheaval that had swept through northern Europe during the previous century? And yet, that upheaval of long ago had no place in today's society, had it not? Moreover, were they not each and every one of them Christians? Did they not share the same values? Did they not love their king, their country, and their children?

Even Delpech could not refute that certain points appeared to tip the balance in favour of a return to the established church. But then, what about the papal artifices, the sacraments, the unchristian worship of artefacts?

It was not until four hours had passed that intendant de la Berchère stood once again before the assembly to conclude with his characteristic gravity.

He said: 'So, my Lords and gentlemen, this morning, we have mutually identified that there is not sufficient difference between our religious values for you to remain separated from the fold. With God's grace and in the name of Christ, who died for us all on the cross, we would willingly embrace you back into our spiritual family here now. But, it is for you to decide: your future lies with your conscience. Let me remind you, however, that you will be rewarded if you adhere to our king's will. On the other hand, if you do not, you will expose yourselves, by your own obstinacy, to the rigours of our soldiers. In which case the winter will be long, I can assure you.'

The Marquis de Boufflers, who had been standing with one foot on his chair, stepped forward. He had ridden back to Montauban the previous evening. He did not want to miss this rendezvous with history. And he did not want history to take a wrong turn. For he knew full well he was not only defending his glorious majesty, he was acting for the good of the nation, of generations to come, and for the sake of future civil peace in France. Had the past not already shown there could only be one religion?

He cleared his throat, and spoke with his characteristic flourish of the hand, though his words were no less uncompromising.

'Indeed, my Lords and gentlemen, if you elect not to reciprocate our embrace, and so do not desire to side with our king, then you shall not be his friends. And you know what soldiers can be like when lodged at the expense of the enemy.'

The intendant continued: 'So, I invite you to step forward now and sign the declaration. You will then be led to the bishop's palace, where you will be given absolution, after which you will recover your status and the full rights of your station.'

The intendant's eyes fleetingly fell upon the respected lawyer and leading member of the assembly, Maître Pierre Satur, standing near the front. After so much heated debate, an intense silence now filled the room. Even for the intendant, it was a tense moment.

De Boufflers, however, knew from experience that the

hush that followed meant that the assembly was collectively bordering on the ledge of their conscience. In other words, they were making up their minds.

At last Maître Satur bowed his head solemnly, then stepped forward. The marquis and the intendant were about to greet him at the register as if he were a friend who had just made it across a ravine on a dangerous footbridge, when a voice rose up from amid the assembly. It was Jacob Delpech who, waving his felt hat, called out: 'Maître, you of all people cannot surely abjure your religion so easily. You are letting down your fellow townsmen.'

The intendant frowned, but it was the marquis who was quickest to react. He said: 'Sir, is it intolerance that prompts you to place your own choice above Maître Satur's conscience?'

'It is common sense and our mutual faith,' said Jacob, who now found himself standing in a little isle of space in the middle of the assembly. 'And with all due respect, my Lords, would you accept someone who so easily renounces his religion for another? If so, then should you not fear that the same person might forfeit your religion just as easily for that of an infidel aggressor?'

This time, it was the intendant, remaining calm and collected in his black satin jerkin, who said: 'We are neither Turks nor Saracens. Your townsman is as much a Christian as we are.'

Jacob beseeched, 'Maître Satur, Sir, have you decided to betray yourself, your fellows, and God?'

The intendant could hardly believe his ears: the impertinent man was going to ruin everything. He was tempted to summon a guard to throw the imbecile out.

Thankfully, however, Pierre Satur, in his ill-fitting periwig, at last turned and answered.

'On the contrary, Sir,' he said, 'the well-being of the people I represent weighs heavy on my conscience. Does it yours?' Excellent answer, thought the intendant. The lawyer continued sternly: 'Even if I had to live with my own betrayal, as you put it, I would not stand here and knowingly risk being responsible for another Saint Bartholomew!'

That was not so good, thought the intendant. Especially as today was the one hundred and thirteenth anniversary of the Protestant massacres by Catholics. However, putting the finger on some people's unspoken fear in fact turned out to be a clincher. To Jacob's dismay, other high-ranking members of the assembly stepped forward in support of Satur.

The balance was thus tipped. In twos and threes, the Huguenots advanced to sign the declaration and their subsequent conversion. Over one hundred and sixty-three abjurations were registered in one fell swoop.

A coup de grace for Protestant resistance in France. Any remonstrance from the likes of Jacob Delpech would thereon be met with scolding stares, disapproving frowns, and scathing words, borne of a sentiment of guilt and bourgeois clannism.

Lefranc de Lacary declared the session closed. With de Boufflers in high spirits and the intendant suppressing a secret smile at the corners of his mouth, the bureau president led the procession of new Catholics to the episcopal palace.

His Eminence the bishop greeted the converts with solemnity and benevolence befitting such a moment of reunification. He gave them absolution in the chapel, and then wisely sent them home for a lunch respite before the afternoon celebrations.

*

News of the conversions spread even before the bells of Saint Jacques could finish their celebratory chimes. The intendant took pleasure once again in his detached observations and superior knowledge of human nature. As he had predicted, after the conversion of the top business and juridical individuals, there came a surge of abjurations which continued throughout the afternoon and all through the ensuing days.

Bishop Jean-Baptiste-Michel was obliged to recruit extra priests from the countryside to cope with the thousands of abjurations. It could only be an act of God. To prove his devotion and to consolidate the new sheep into the flock, he orchestrated a great procession which meandered through town singing a Te Deum in thanksgiving.

All reformist obstructions having thus been removed, Montauban could breathe again and resume business as before. It was in general a time of relief, and one that came with the perspective of renewed prosperity. Printers could print, journalists could report, and solicitors and clerks could return to their offices. The time of persecution had ended that Friday, 24th August. Except, that is, for the recalcitrant, as the intendant labelled them. He would now be able to focus on weeding them out.

6

25 August 1685

MONSIEUR BOUDOIN, A red-faced, portly man in his late forties, was one Montalbanais who had welcomed the dragonnade.

Every day since it began, he had given thanks in prayer for God's mysterious ways that had brought him out of the clutches of debt and ruin. He had lost much of his wife's inheritance investing in slaves for the New World, whose ship had sunk off the coast of Barbados. He had spent many a night bent over, worrying how he could avoid the shame of selling his house, and having to take rented accommodation at the age of forty-eight.

Was the dragonnade a godsend?

At any rate, he would certainly not miss such windows of opportunity so close to home. He knew he had to get in quick, though; hesitation would only lead to picking up the leftovers. He had been diligently busying himself across town by purchasing Huguenot furniture from soldiers so they could buy victuals. In this way, Monsieur Boudoin also had the moral satisfaction of defusing a potentially explosive situation which could put the Huguenots in mortal danger, for there was nothing more hazardous than lodging angry men of war.

He had nonetheless been shy if not embarrassed about helping his wealthy heretic neighbour—a neighbour who also happened to be one of his creditors. However, with the recent abjurations en masse, those windows of opportunity throughout the town were now closing with surprising rapidity. Nobody would have guessed in a thousand years that catholicisation could be achieved so quickly in the Protestant stronghold. It just went to show what little mettle this generation of Protestant bourgeois was made of. Soldiers were relinquishing their quarters at a horrendous rate, and with a dwindling number of Huguenots, Monsieur Boudoin had no choice but to endeavour to put his scruples to one side with regard to his neighbour, Monsieur Delpech.

Jacob's pantry had been emptied of food three times by the fifth afternoon of the soldiers' arrival. To pay for present and future upkeep, Lieutenant Ducamp resolved to sell the dining-room suite, four walnut armchairs with a matching low table in the latest fashion, an escritoire handed down from Jacob's grandfather, a fine Venetian cabinet, and a beautiful leather-topped ministerial desk. The lieutenant had no idea where to sell the bourgeois junk, and only had a rough idea of what it was worth. Thankfully, Monsieur Boudoin from across the road was at hand with ready cash, which would save Ducamp's men from having to lug furniture across town to the auction room.

*

When they saw the thick-armed soldiers envisaging how to carry the furniture outside, Monsieur and Madame Delpech voiced their outrage.

'Sir, you are breaking the law,' said Jacob to Lieutenant Ducamp, who was pulling up his brown-leather thigh boot. He had been giving his feet a breather. Jacob continued, 'If you insist in your endeavours, then I shall have no other choice than to inform the authorities!'

'Not my onions, pal,' said Ducamp, stamping his heel to the bottom of his boot. He turned and barked another order at his men, who were passing the large table through the dining-room door that led to the entrance hall. 'Easy, boys,' he said, 'that's good stuff; we don't wanna scratch it.'

Didier Ducamp proceeded to carry out his plan as if the owners were of no consequence, a delicious tactic he had picked up in Bearn as part of the strategy to pressure the Huguenots into submission and abjuration. It usually worked wonders, far better than any string of insults, although insults did generally have to come first as a preamble since they set the tone.

Madame Delpech, who had staggered to a seat among her children, was promptly lifted up by her underarms so that the soldier could carry the embroidered armchair outside. Jacob protested, and took his wife's shaking hand.

Ducamp turned to them, and in his deep baritone voice, he said calmly: 'Abjure. And we will put everything back, and leave you in peace.'

'Intimidation will not get you what you want,' said Jacob, staring back with determination in his eyes.

Jeanne, with new courage, said, 'What God gives, no man can take away.'

Ducamp wondered for a moment if they feigned a lack of common sense. Or were they just being plain arrogant because of his station as a lowly lieutenant? He decided to raise the stakes and told a soldier to fetch the carved oak crib from the master bedchamber. Ducamp knew it was customary to lay infants in the ancestral cot passed down through the ages, and by the looks of it, the one upstairs was no exception.

Jeanne had laid all her children in that crib, and had prepared it for her new baby.

Ducamp looked straight into her eyes; he knew he had every chance of winning an abjuration if he could break the woman.

But she stood her ground with bourgeois dignity. She said, 'Naked came I out of my mother's womb, and naked shall I return: the Lord gave, and the Lord hath taken away.'

Ducamp was again struck in his pride. His game of one-upmanship had done nothing more than lock the Huguenots further into their stubborn defiance.

An hour later, most of the furniture was stacked in the street. Before accepting Boudoin's ludicrous offer, Ducamp decided he would give Delpech and his duchess one last chance.

'For God's sake, man,' he said to Jacob. There was a slight resonance now in the bare dining room where they stood. 'Why don't you just lie? Then you can have everything back. You are not signing away your life, you know.'

'But you see, Sir,' said Jacob, 'we would be doing precisely that. We would be signing away our values, our faith in God, and His promise of eternal life.'

Ducamp knew now for sure that the man would not be subjugated. It was a waste of time trying; he had seen the obstinate type before in Pau.

Jacob continued, 'If you go ahead with this travesty of justice, which amounts to nothing less than pillaging, then I shall have to report it to your commander . . .'

Ducamp shrugged; he had heard it all before. He let the Huguenot rattle off his foolish protest while he strode outside, where a crowd of onlookers wes already admiring the fine furniture. Then he went ahead with the sale.

*

Jacob did not wish to leave Jeanne and their children at the mercy of ruthless hands, so he accompanied them most of the way to Jeanne's sister's on foot. Their coach had been rendered unusable, and their servants had fled. Given the ardent appetites of the men who would not have thought twice about taking even old Monique, neither Jacob nor Jeanne could blame the servants for leaving the house. It was, on the contrary, one worry less.

Once past Place des Monges, which led on to Rue Porte du Moustier where his sister-in-law lived, Jeanne let him head back towards the town hall, where he hoped to gain an audience with the Marquis de Boufflers.

The balmy streets were throbbing with bells chiming, drums thumping, processional singing, and most of all, the clopping and clatter of horses and soldiers departing. They were vacating their lodgements and joining their regiment across the river Tarn at their base camp in Villebourbon.

Jeanne had barely walked ten paces when she came upon a notice freshly pasted to a tree. It announced a fine of 500 livres to anyone found guilty of harbouring persons of the so-called Reformed religion.

From the corner of the street lined with elms, she saw

soldiers on the steps of her sister's house. Her heart sank; she did not want to bring further distress upon her sister's household. Despite the discomfort of her load, she turned around, and with her children holding her skirts, she headed back towards her house, where she hoped Jacob would have returned by the time she arrived.

It was not, however, the distance that pained her most. She could take her time, and besides, she felt that the longer she could keep herself and her children from those dreadful soldiers, the better. No, it was not her breathlessness nor her aching back that gave her the most discomfort: it was the number of remarks directed at her from houses she passed along the way. Folk of the 'true' religion, now in the majority and with the tacit connivance of local authorities, openly vented their disapproval of nonconformists.

Jeanne, her three children now strung along behind her, entered Rue Larrazet, a quiet, narrow lane lined with tall houses that bypassed the pomp and procession now in Rue Soubirou on the north side of Place des Monges. It was a route she used to take in the hottest months of summer when she was younger.

*

In an upstairs room halfway up the narrow street, despite the late hour of the day, two young chambermaids were still doing the bedrooms.

'I heard the baron say we are living in an historic moment,' said the new girl from Toulouse while tucking in the bed linen. She had only been with the house since the beginning of summer. She had agreed to go there because of the extra pay for Catholic servants, and perhaps because the baron had a penchant for fair hair.

'That may be, Elise, but we've still got to change the linen, sweep the floors, and empty the pots,' said the other chambermaid, whose name was Yvette. She was not yet twenty, slightly younger than Elise, though more serious-minded under her mop of sauerkraut hair.

'I thought we'd never get through all that washing-up. And the mess . . .'

'After-procession festivities,' said Yvette, flopping the bolster pillow like a black pudding across the bed. 'Went on late into the night, you can be sure.'

'The baron was ever so tipsy,' Elise said coquettishly as she picked up the chamber pot. Moving to the window, she said, 'I heard him say good times are here to stay.'

She placed the pot on top of an oak chest of drawers and leaned out of the half-shuttered window. 'Quick!' she said, turning back to Yvette. 'Here comes that Delpech woman. Looks like 'er old man's gone and dumped her. Poor thing, she's red as a cardinal. Lovely dress, though.'

Yvette joined her at the window and said, 'I don't pity her at all, nor her sect. They all stick together like shit to a sheet. Huh, think they're more saintly than the pope, they do.'

Elise said, 'Not anymore they don't, though, do they, ha!'

'Glad they've banned it at last,' said Yvette.

'Took 'em long enough, didn't it?'

'But she still won't convert back, you know,' said Yvette. 'Thinks she's a cut above the rest. Huh, we'll soon see where her airs and graces get her now.'

'And what of her children? Has she a heart?'

'Her sort only thinks of themselves!'

'Huguenot nobs are no different from our lot, then,' said Elise with her characteristic little laugh.

'And they're the devil incarnate when it comes to affairs. You know Monsieur Boudoin, the odds and sods merchant, who fell on hard times?'

'Yeah.'

'Well, he says her husband offered to lend him money, at an exorbitant rate too. So much so that he ended up having to borrow more and more just to pay back the interest.'

'That's not very Christian-like, is it?' said Elise. 'Glad there ain't no Huguenots in Toulouse: we kicked 'em all out. If you can't fit in, then ship out. That's what my gran says!'

'No,' said Yvette, 'you can't fit a square peg into a round hole, can ya?'

'The baron says the bishop has been so patient, and so forgiving.'

'He's a saintly man,' said Yvette, 'a bon vivant but saintly. Yet the likes of her will show him no gratitude. They ought to send her to the nunnery.'

Elise pushed open the shutter another few inches with one hand and took up the chamber pot with the other. 'Take that, heretic bitch!' she yelled out and threw the pot's contents out of the window. She pulled the shutter flap back with a playful but guilty little giggle.

'Elise, you didn't!' said Yvette, stepping away from the window.

'I did, right on her bonce too.'

'That's rotten.'

'No, it i'n't, it's patriotic. And don't look so glum, it's only a bit of fun. Won't be able to do it when she turns Catholic, will we!'

'Good shot, though,' conceded Yvette, who suddenly realised that the new girl was capable of anything, and wondered if she had already obliged the baron.

*

Jeanne walked on without showing her disgust, thankful that the chamber pot water had splashed her coif, not her children.

She made it back to her house as the church bell struck four o'clock. But Jacob was not there, and neither were the soldiers. So she now stood outside her own home with no key. She thanked God she had thought to take some *pain d'épices*, which she broke and shared among her children.

Her condition and her situation touched the heart of a neighbour, Madame Simon, a pious Catholic woman of fifty-six. It may have been forbidden to offer shelter to a Huguenot, but she was not about to watch a pregnant woman suffer from the arrogant stupidity of men. She brought her a chair and some fresh lemon juice, which Jeanne accepted with overflowing gratitude. Had she been obliged to stand anymore, her legs and back would have given way under the strain.

*

Jacob's venture to file a complaint had not met with greater success than Jeanne's attempt at finding refuge. De Boufflers, sensing that the wind of change was favourable, had lost no time in giving the order to a unit of troops to embark on another missionary tour of the neighbouring townships and villages. Lieutenant Ducamp and his dragoons were among these men. Now that the capital of the generality had fallen, the marquis was determined to convert the rest of Lower Quercy. And he could not wait to see the king's face, not to mention that of Madame de Maintenon.

In the absence of the marquis, Jacob had insisted on seeing the intendant. But de la Berchère refused him an audience. Instead, he sent Delpech an order to return to his house, to greet another dispatch of the king's soldiers.

On arriving back home, Delpech was astonished to discover his wife desperately fanning herself on a chair, and his children, Lizzie and Paul playing, Lulu sleeping, on the stone threshold of his front door. He deduced the soldiers must have left and taken the key.

He was contemplating how to break into his own premises when a magistrate appeared with the key and a note from Lieutenant Ducamp.

As they entered the spacious townhouse, even the magistrate was unable to hide his dismay at the disorder. They were met with the scattering of vermin and bottles rolling on floorboards, splashes of wine on every textile, broken glass and scraps of food trodden into the beautifully woven carpet, grease wiped on the curtains, and not a stick of furniture in the large dining room other than a two-seater sofa and a solitary crib.

'If you will, Sir,' said Jacob, determined to muffle his emotions, 'I would ask you to record the state in which you find my property.'

'I am sorry, Sir,' replied the magistrate, recovering his mask of stoicism. 'That is not within my remit.'

After the civil servant took his leave, Jacob opened the note from the lieutenant and read.

'I fear my men were lambs compared to your next guests.

You will have been warned. If you love your children, ABJURE!'

*

The interval would no doubt be short, thought Jeanne. So she quickly assembled her children in her bedchamber, laid out fresh clothes for them, and did likewise for herself.

While changing her youngest daughter, she could not help asking herself why on earth she did not leave the country when she had been offered the chance. But she knew she must not give in to remorse, and besides, at least she was with her husband.

The sound of the door latch brought her out of her ponderings.

'Paul, where are you going?' she said to her seven-year-old boy, who was about to disappear into the corridor.

'To the privy, Mama,' he said, and she waved him on, telling him not to dawdle.

She refocused her attention on dressing Louise—barely three and already as chatty as a magpie—and tried not to think about the conditions under which she might have to go into labour. Instead, she forced herself to remain confident that God would light their lantern. Be it through feminine intuition or God's grace, she then turned her mind to preparing a small leather travel bag with the bare necessities.

*

Downstairs, the boy trundled through the kitchen towards the courtyard where the new latrine pit was housed. Jacob was dipping a finger into the copper basin of water he had

55

been heating up for Jeanne. It was the first time the boy had seen his father in front of a stove, and he concluded that he looked perfectly odd in a kitchen. But with the house now empty of servants, Jacob had been given no choice. At least it had allowed him time to mull over his harvest plans, which he hoped to send to his overseer in Verlhac.

He was about to stoke the fire again when a heavy rapping at the front door announced the dreaded new arrivals.

'Come here, my boy,' he said to Paul. He had grabbed a leather jug which he now only partially filled so it would not be too heavy. With one hand around his son's shoulder, he carried the jug to the foot of the stairs, where he handed it to the boy.

'Take it up to your mother quick as you can,' he said. The boy took the leather jug with both hands. 'Think you can manage?'

'Yes, Papa,' said Paul.

Of course he could manage, and he made it his personal mission to deliver it to his mother. He heaved the receptacle up the stairs, letting it rest just an instant on every third step.

The soldiers were now banging on the front door with a hard instrument, probably the butt of a musket.

'Open up, by order of the king!' yelled a deep voice through the three-inch oak door. Jacob could no longer stall and soon found himself face to face with the soldier who introduced himself as Lieutenant Godefroi Rapier. Despite being a doorstep lower, the lieutenant looked square into Jacob's eyes as he handed him a billet.

He said: 'You are Monsieur Delpech, merchant and proprietor of this house?'

'I am,' said Jacob.

'You are to give full board and lodging to eight soldiers now, and six more this evening,' said the lieutenant as Jacob perused the billet. Jacob glanced back at the rugged, unshaven face, and the soldier said: 'Unless you have decided to abjure.'

'I have not,' said Jacob. 'I am afraid I shall have to let you in.'

The soldier pushed his way into the house, closely followed by a rabble of men of arms. They were not amused to find the storeroom bare of meat, and the most movable furniture gone.

'Sir,' said Jacob, 'the previous soldiers took everything I had; I cannot be made responsible for their pillaging. There is not much left I can give you.'

At that moment, the sound of a jug clunking on the floorboards upstairs alerted the lieutenant.

'Bertrand, Lecoq, go see upstairs!'

Jacob explained that the noise was only his son taking water to his pregnant wife, but the lieutenant continued as if he had not been interrupted.

'Monsieur Delpech, I am in possession of an inventory of your properties. I do declare that we shall have no choice but to proceed in the sale of the livestock from your farms.'

*

Paul was desperately trying to carry the jug with two hands down the long, high-ceilinged corridor towards his parents' bedroom.

'You, boy, stop there!' ordered the soldier named Bertrand. Paul halted a second, but then carried on, straight as a post and tightening the muscles in his buttocks. He

57

realised, however, that he was not going to make it. And there was something else. He let drop the jug and still kept walking with a stiff gait, tears welling in his eyes.

'Pwah,' said Lecoq, as he approached the boy. 'Little tyke's gone and shit himself.'

This gave cause for much laughter among the soldiers. Lecoq grabbed the jug and threw the contents at the boy's lower body, where soft poo was running down his leg.

The banging at the front door had prompted Jeanne to make herself decent. She was passing her robe battante over her bump when she heard the ruckus outside her room. The next instant, two soldiers burst in, one holding her son by the scruff of the neck.

'Looks like the lady's been bitten by a mosquito, Henri,' said Lecoq, nudging his brother-in-arms, who looked sternly at Jeanne and said forcefully, 'We are requisitioning this room by order of the king. So, lady, take your heretic brats downstairs before we chuck 'em out the window!'

'Unless you'd care to abjure,' added Lecoq in a show of civility.

*

Scuttling from storeroom to dining room, Jacob was at pains to accommodate his visitors, who wanted feeding at once.

'What will you give us to sell to procure more food?' demanded Lieutenant Rapier, angry with hunger.

'I told you, I can give you nothing but what is left in the pantry.'

'What, stinking cheese?' roared the lieutenant. 'If you're trying to be funny, I am not laughing! Where d'you keep your money?'

'I have none here, Sir.'

'You lie,' said Rapier, who then motioned for Jacob to follow him into the study, and to a subordinate, he pointed out the bookcase which contained no fewer than two hundred and sixty-three leather-bound books. From experience, he knew Huguenots could be deceitfully devious. 'Guillaume,' he blasted, 'look inside them books, then tear every one of 'em apart!'

Jacob protested that there were no hollowed books for hiding coins in his collection; it would be a sacrilege to destroy them.

'The Huguenot has a point: they're worth more in one piece,' said the lieutenant. 'Once you've checked them, stack 'em outside where people can buy 'em. They'll fetch enough to keep us in grub and grog till we sell his cattle.'

Jacob's further protestations fell on deaf ears.

Rapier went to continue his tour of the premises, but then turned back to Delpech and said: 'Oh, nearly forgot: given that Monsieur de Molinier, our previous host, abjured, you'll notice your billet's been dated to include payment for our time spent at his residence.'

*

Monsieur Boudoin had strategically placed his favourite armchair in front of a first-floor window so that he could observe any comings and goings at the big house—a house which he no longer saw as a source of debt anxiety, but as a beacon of hope—in case he had to step in to temper any potentially volatile situation.

He had heard of how obnoxious men of war could become on empty stomachs. It was neighbourly help of a kind, he thought to himself; it saved them from physical suffering, and you could not take your possessions with you to the next world, could you? Such was the purport of Monsieur Boudoin's musings when he saw beautiful leather-bound books being piled up outside the house.

They did not have to wait there long before Monsieur Boudoin appeared with a ready cash offer, so that the soldiers could fetch some venison and bread and fill their cups with wine. Boudoin was only too glad to be able to help facilitate the cohabitation, despite the fact that his ground-floor storage space was seriously running out of room, which was worrying. He would have to rent somewhere to harbour his growing stock of household items and furniture. The soldiers soon became busy with their book-delivery task, which, upon Boudoin's suggestion, was extended to Jacob's collection of paintings and tapestries.

Jeanne took advantage of the brief hiatus to clean Paul down in the courtyard. Jacob had managed to retrieve some fresh breeches for the boy. While dressing him, Jeanne whispered to her husband that she could not have her baby in her home now, filled as it was with such callous individuals.

'I am unworthy,' said Jacob, who had taken his youngest daughter from the arms of Elizabeth. He kissed her forehead, then turned back to his wife. 'I am a wretch who cannot even offer protection to his children, nor comfort to his wife in her greatest hour of need.'

'You have done all you can, Jacob,' said Jeanne, and, preferring to make a joke out of their predicament, she said, 'I mean, you did heat up the water!'

Jacob's face momentarily lost all sign of strain when he

said, 'Yes, it was quite an operation.' The children half-giggled at the thought of their father in the kitchen.

In a graver tone, Jeanne then said, 'The truth is, it is not your fault, Jacob. It was I who insisted on coming to town, against your wishes.'

Jacob said in a lower voice, 'They are requisitioning the farms and the country house. Where will you go?'

'God will show us a way,' said Jeanne.

'But you have no means of transport. And how will you get past the soldiers?'

'Keep your faith, Jacob,' said Jeanne softly. 'I simply sense it would be dangerous for the children to remain here much longer.'

It was not like Jeanne to use exaggerated language, and Jacob was suddenly struck with horror at the unspecified danger. He wanted them to remain close by him where he could at least try to protect them, with his life if necessary. But then what? However, before they could reach the outcome of their whispered conversation, it was rudely curtailed when the lieutenant stepped into the yard and stood before them.

He said: 'There's no place for pregnant women in a soldier's quarters. Your wench and her sprats will have to go!' He strode on towards the privy at the opposite side of the courtyard.

'But, Sir,' said Jacob, almost unable to process the barbaric command. Handing his daughter back to Lizzy, he continued, 'My wife is on the verge of childbirth. This is her lawful home.' Rapier halted in his stride and turned back to Jacob, who was saying, 'Is this no longer a state of law where an honest man can live in peace in his own home?'

'Not for you, it ain't,' said the lieutenant. 'This is a Catholic country. You've got five minutes, or I'll kick 'em out myself. And by the way, you're coming with me to sell your livestock.'

Rapier continued to the privy. At the door, he turned back and shouted: 'Where's your god now, eh? Five minutes.' Then, after a beat, he added: 'Unless you abjure!' before disappearing inside the brick outhouse.

Jeanne looked at her husband with courage. 'At least we are settled,' she said. Jacob took her in his arms, and they reached for their three children, who had huddled around them.

Feeling inside his jacket, in a whisper Jacob said: 'Take this, conceal it.'

Jeanne took the pouch of gold coins he had furtively unhitched from his inner pocket and slipped it inside her dress.

A few minutes later, she felt a twinge of fear and despair as she led her children over the threshold of their home. However, she plucked up the instant she perceived her neighbour, who feigned to be engrossed in a book. She would not, for the life of her, let him believe she was beaten.

*

Jeanne's back, hips, and pelvis ached continuously, and stabbing pains in her abdomen had her reaching for a wall or a tree.

She had walked first to the west side of town to the house of her mother-in-law, the widow of a respected physician. But a neighbour had told her that the old lady had taken her coach with her daughter and had not been seen since.

She had wended her way back across town, avoiding the busiest thoroughfares. In Rue Porte du Moustier, she laid down a blanket over a stone bench just twenty yards from her sister's house, where troopers were still quartered.

Paul, in spite of his years, could not bear the indignity and shame of his mother having to give birth in the open street. He still remembered the screams from the birth of the last baby called Jérôme, who went to heaven not long after his baptism. When the church bell chimed seven o'clock, the boy took up all his courage—which was greater than his recent embarrassment and fear—and ran to his aunt's house, despite his mother calling him back. He hoped the soldiers would be eating and that a servant would come to the door.

Instead of a servant, it turned out to be an old man with cropped grey hair who resembled his kind-hearted uncle, Robert.

'Paul, my lad,' said the man, keeping his voice down. It was obvious to the boy now that this old man was his uncle, whom he had never seen without his big hair. And how much older he looked compared to the other day when they were playing at swords in the garden.

Robert Garrisson needed no explanation. A glance across the street to his left told him everything he needed to know.

'Step inside, my lad,' he said.

'We have nowhere to go, Mother can no longer walk about, and my little sister keeps crying,' said Paul, standing inside the carriage entrance where a sedan chair was parked.

Robert made a sign for his nephew to stay put. Then he climbed the flagstone steps, and disappeared through a first-floor door into a room filled with the tumult of men of war, eating, grunting, hollering, drinking, burping, and laughing.

Five minutes later, the boy was chomping into a chicken drumstick while telling his aunt Suzanne how they had been told to leave their own house.

'She must come inside, Robert,' said Suzanne, holding a clenched hand to her lips.

'Not yet, my dear, the soldiers here will send her away too. Then where will she go?'

'But she cannot have her baby in the street like an animal!'

'God forbid, no. There is only one way, Suzanne, and may God forgive what I am about to do.' Robert then turned to his nephew. 'Paul, I want you to tell your mother to endeavour to move further up the street, a few houses past our own in that direction,' he said, pointing the way. 'Do you understand?'

'Yes, my uncle,' said the boy.

'Tell her to wait there until the soldiers have left this house. Your aunt will let her know when you can come inside.'

*

It took all of Jeanne's strength to move the thirty yards up the street, where she was able to place her blanket on a convenient tree stump.

There, she prayed to God that her labour pains would not intensify until she had found a refuge. She stroked her son's hair (his head was on her lap) and rocked her three-year-old daughter, who had fallen asleep now that she had been given food and drink from the basket of provisions that Paul had brought from their aunt Suzanne's.

At that hour of the day, most folk were having their

supper; only a handful of passers-by walked the street. Of those who did, only a few gave a look of surprise at the sight of a well-clad family huddled there without the father. They mostly went on their way as if nothing were there at all. Others crossed the road, grumbling their disgust at the thought that some deserters still dared give resistance to the king and the church of Rome.

The clock had scarcely struck quarter past eight when the door opened. An officer stepped out of the Garrissons' house. On his heels came Robert, who was in turn followed by half a dozen red-faced dragoons, some put out at having to leave their comfortable quarters. Robert pointed to his left to detract the officer's attention away from Jeanne and her children, waiting further up the street to the right. The section of soldiers went marching down the road.

As soon as the last bonneted head turned the corner, Suzanne came running out of her house. Jeanne managed to get to her feet on her approach. Then, for the first time since the overt persecution began, she let her emotions get the better of her, and she wept in the arms of her sister.

*

'I know what Robert has done,' said Jeanne, once within the safety of the house.

However, for the time being, Suzanne was not open to discussion and focused on getting her sister up the second flight of stairs and into bed. Elizabeth was given instructions to prepare whatever she could find to eat for her siblings. Antoine, the valet, was sent to fetch Madame Gauberte, the midwife.

'Robert has abjured, hasn't he?' said Jeanne.

65

'Do not worry your sweet soul, my dear sister,' said Suzanne in her characteristic mirthful tone, despite her uncharacteristically ruffled appearance. 'Yes, Robert has abjured; I have not, though. The soldiers have gone, and you, my dear, are safe now.'

'But it is my doing . . .'

'Nonsense. Robert wants me to tell you that he did it not only so that you could have your baby in appropriate surroundings, but because he is not a young man anymore. He could not have endured the chaos and suffering from the soldiers much longer.'

'But if I had not come—'

'No buts, just listen. He wants you to know that your coming has liberated him. It has given him an honest reason to abjure, at least on paper, though not in his soul. So, my sister, I implore you to rest: you must focus all your strength on the baby and the work at hand. I shall make the preparations.'

7

26 and 27 August 1685

WITH RESTRAINED FERVOUR, de la Berchère said: 'I shall send a note to Versailles with the news that Montauban is once again a Catholic city.'

'Nine thousand six hundred and ninety conversions,' said the bishop, sitting back in his leather-padded armchair, thoroughly sated. 'And not a drop of blood spilled!'

'The method is simply ingenious.'

'A miracle.'

'Yes, quite. A miracle,' said the intendant. Indeed, it was as though the good Lord had smiled down upon them. He would say just that in his letter to the king. Although, as he then pointed out, it was true that they did have the advantage of an army behind them.

'Guided by the grace of God,' intoned the bishop, whose prayers had been answered completely. There could not have been a greater reward for his relentless struggle against heresy, and he inwardly praised the Lord every minute of the day. All his doubts had been dispelled.

They were sitting on either side of the long, polished oak table in the middle of the intendant's chamber. It might have seemed like they were enjoying a hearty meal, but in fact they were busy totalling the piles of signed abjuration certificates against the number of absolutions performed. This meant tallying the totals given by the country priests who had been assigned to churches, and strategic points throughout the town, to meet the staggering demand.

Their conversation was interrupted by a knock at the door. On the intendant's command, the clerk entered. 'I thought you should know that the Delpech woman is reported to have been taken in by her sister, Sir,' he said servilely. 'Yet, the sister's husband, Maître Robert Garrisson, is a newly converted Catholic.'

'Then we shall have to fine Monsieur Garrisson five hundred livres as dictates the law,' said de la Berchère with a resolute frown. 'If he insists on putting her up, he must be imprisoned, and the woman thrown out by force.'

'Yes, my Lord.' The clerk gave a slow, deliberate bow.

'If I may, my Lord,' said the bishop. Lifting his hand from its natural resting place on his belly, he propped himself up squarely in his wide armchair and said, 'It might ignite public feeling if we did not allow her off the streets to have her child. Indeed, I have been led to believe that some of the new Catholics are already regretting their conversion. An incident of this sort could well kindle a feeling of indignation and cause some of them to rebel, or worse, to revert back to their sect.'

'Hmm, you have a point, Monseigneur,' said the intendant, arching his long, spindly fingers towards his nose in a pose of contemplation. 'Indeed, my informants tell me that some are already endeavouring to leave the realm.'

'What is more, my Lord, there have been more male than

female converts. Women are easily given to their emotions and could rally to her side, which could create further imbalance.'

'In that case, let her have her baby,' said the intendant to the clerk. 'Then do as the law dictates.'

The clerk bowed once more and left the room.

*

Jacob had been relegated to manservant in his own home. He was allowed only to sit in the entrance hall, where every time he closed his eyes, a soldier belched out his name, or an insult, followed by a command.

'Jacob, more wine!'

'Jacob, more chicken!'

'Shit-face Jacob, fetch the pisspot!'

However, it was night-time and the tall house had fallen into relative silence. Even his guard had overindulged in the excellent wine, and was at present slouched over, snoring heavily on the wooden bench in the hall beside him.

Jacob sat there a moment longer, his thoughts with his wife and children, but also with his production and his trade. Should he tell Jeanne that he had invested a large sum of money in Satur's last venture? That they were without news, that quite likely the ship had sunk with his debtor in it? There again, did it matter now that he was on the verge of losing everything anyway?

It was two days since his wife and children had been turned out of their own home. Word had reached him that it had pleased God to give Jeanne a refuge. And the previous evening, Robert Garrisson had sent him word of the birth of a baby girl.

All was peaceful; he could even hear mice in the next room, rummaging over the venison carcass parts and sleeping bodies of soldiers. At last the time had come for him to slip out.

Under a crescent moon, he hurried through the empty streets of Montauban to the Garrissons' house, where he found a welcome respite from servitude. He immediately recovered some human warmth, and some of the dignity that the soldiers had been steadily grinding away.

He lost no time in kissing his children, all four of them, and his wife, before letting her close her weary eyes while he held her hand.

Before falling deep into slumber in the soft four-poster bed, Jeanne recalled the first birth, how he held her hand until she slept, and how he was still holding it when she awoke two hours later for the feed. She remembered how he marvelled at the endless supply from her breasts, nature's fountain, she remembered him calling it.

Tonight, however, his visit would have to be brief. The soldiers might stir at any moment, even though he had taken the precaution of lacing the barrel of his best wine with sweet oil of vitriol, a strong sedative that he had found in the medicine chest inherited from his father.

'A simple signature on a piece of paper will not take away my religion,' said Robert at the dining-room table, which was lit up by a twelve-candle chandelier. Jacob had noticed the room was missing silverware and candelabras, but at least the lawyer had saved his furniture. And his paintings of family members still hung on the four walls above the oak panelling.

'Quite so,' said Jacob, spreading smooth duck pâté over

a crust of bread. 'But you have abjured all the same. Indeed, with all due respect, Robert, I believe you have made yourself a wealthier man by your simple signature.'

'You could do the same, Jacob,' said Robert, who sat without eating. 'Abjure and lie low until the time is right to leave. Or until the king dies, upon my soul!'

'I cannot.'

'A lie to gain time. That is all.'

'I cannot put aside my faith as you put aside your convictions inside a court of law!'

'That is unfair. I have never defended anybody I thought unworthy of a second chance.'

'Well, now I am the one who risks losing everything, while you and Satur sign your abjurations and benefit from the exoneration of this year's tithe.'

'My signature also means your wife did not give birth in the street, Jacob.'

'And I am eternally grateful, Robert. Perhaps I am being unfair. But if everyone in the country has the same response, there will officially be no more Protestants in France, then I fear the worst.'

'The revocation of the Edict of Nantes, you mean. I am sure that is what the king has intended. In which case you must flee, my dear friend, to a more clement country. And do not be surprised if I join you. Many have already fled to Geneva, Amsterdam, Berlin, and even to London.'

'I doubt my seafaring legs would get me across Lake Geneva, let alone the Channel. Nevertheless, it is also my view that we should flee. But the realm is sealed, never mind the city gates . . .'

A commotion in the corridor cut their conversation

short. Then Suzanne swept into the room.

'Robert, Jacob, soldiers are coming!'

'So be it,' said Robert, now standing calm but resolute. Being a lawyer, he knew better than anyone the price to pay for harbouring a Huguenot. 'I will gladly pay the fine.'

'That is not all, if I may, Sir,' said a broad-shouldered man now standing, holding his dented hat in his hands, in the doorway behind Madame Garrisson. His name was Abel Rostan. A few years earlier, Robert had defended his innocence upon a salt-smuggling charge, so saving him from being sentenced to five years on a galley ship. He worked as a caterer, and had been busy with his wife, serving the king's officers in their quarters.

'Do come in, Monsieur Rostan,' said Robert.

'I am your servitor, Sir,' said Rostan with a bow. 'I came as soon as I overheard soldiers grumbling about having to go out at this hour. They are coming here to throw Madame Delpech out of your house, Sir, and yourself in prison if you refuse.'

'So help me God, is there no reprieve from their monstrosities?' said Jacob, standing with his fists on the table.

'I thought this would come,' said Robert. 'In truth, I have been half expecting it.'

He thanked Abel Rostan for his presence of mind and let his valet show him out. Turning back to Jacob, he said, 'I have been thinking about it: we must endeavour to send Jeanne to the country.'

'My properties have been requisitioned, down to the smallest farm.'

'Then she and the children must go to Villemade,' said Suzanne.

'Exactly,' said Robert. 'The farmhouse there, barring the milkmaid, has remained vacant since the farmer and his wife fled the country.' Robert paced to the doorway and called to his valet, who was already on the stairs. 'Antoine, make ready the carriage!'

'I will wake the children,' said Suzanne, who then hurried up the stairs with Jacob behind her.

*

Alerted by the disturbance, Jeanne was already sitting up in the high bed as Jacob walked into her room.

'They are coming, aren't they?' she said calmly.

'Robert is going to take you where you will be safe,' he said, holding her hand.

'You must come as well, Jacob.'

'Yes,' seconded Robert, who had walked in behind his brother-in-law. 'Then as soon as you are fit to travel, you must all leave the country.'

'I cannot go anywhere yet, or they will come looking for me,' said Jacob. 'I must return to our house and pray that by doing so, you and the children may be left in peace.'

Before either Jeanne or Robert could protest, there came a banging at the door downstairs.

'There is no time,' said Suzanne, now standing in the doorway with the three children, still sleepy-eyed in their improvised night clothes.

'Jacob, you'd better leave,' said Robert, who then stepped onto the landing, leaned over the parapet of the stairway, and called to Antoine to join them.

Hurriedly, Jacob kissed his wife and embraced his children while the soldiers banged on the door. He was glad he had not troubled Jeanne with the probable failure of his latest venture. It no longer mattered. And in that confused moment, it occurred to him that he may never see his family again. Yet the urgency of the situation meant he could not dwell.

'Put the children back in their beds,' said Robert to his wife. 'If they are not seen, they will not be missed.' Turning to Jacob, he said, 'Antoine will show you a back way I used to take as a boy; I will vouch for Jeanne. Go now, my friend, before your soldiers wake and find you gone.'

An instant later, Jacob was leaping behind the valet from a rear window onto the stable roof. In the white light of the moon, he then edged along a dividing brick wall to the end, where he jumped down into the alley that led to an adjoining street.

Robert, meanwhile made much ado out of lighting the candles of the wrought-iron sconces and unlocking the coach entrance door to attend to the unwanted visitors. He then tried to stall the soldiers further by discussing the legality of the operation.

'Sir,' he said, still holding his candlestick dripping with wax, 'tell me where the law stipulates that one is not permitted to welcome a close relative into one's house. Madame Delpech is my wife's sister.'

'I don't care if she's the bloody countess of Toulouse. She's a Huguenot, and I have my orders,' said the officer, who bowled past the ageing lawyer, almost knocking him to the ground.

Further into the spacious hall at the bottom of the stairs, he was met by Jeanne Delpech, slowly descending the dimly lit stairway that led to the first-floor living quarters, cradling her baby in her arms.

'Sir,' she said calmly and with dignity. 'I believe you would like me to end my social visit to my sister's.'

'Madame Delpech, I presume,' said the officer, never impressed by high–minded bourgeois manners. 'You should know that heretics are no longer permitted to mingle with true-blooded French folk faithful to their king. You have brought a hefty fine upon this household. You must leave these premises immediately, or this man will face prison.'

'That is ridiculous, man,' said Robert. 'Can't you see she has a newborn infant in her arms?'

'Sir, you yourself have seen sense and have abjured, have you not? Then answer me this: is it not ridiculous, indeed scandalous, to obstinately choose hardship over comfort for one's loved ones? Especially when your child's life is at stake?' It could have been Robert's argument to Jacob. The officer turned to Jeanne. 'You, Madame, you know what you need to do for your hardships to cease. You simply have to sign the abjuration form; that is all. Is that really so hard?'

'Sir, I would rather die in my faith than find momentary comfort in deceit.'

Though he knew her answer was not aimed at him in any way, Robert nonetheless felt its sting of truth. He would have that minute reconverted had it not been for the fact that the only way he could help Jeanne out of the godforsaken city was as a free-moving subject of the king. And that evidently meant adhering to the Roman Catholic Church.

Jeanne continued, 'My soul I surrender to God alone; to our king, I do swear my allegiance.'

The officer, seeing there was no point in trying to make this Huguenot see reason, directed two of his men to accompany her to the open front door.

Jeanne was marching calmly before a line of five soldiers when her sister came scuttling down the stairs.

'Sir,' she said. 'I beseech you to allow Madame the decency of privacy. Please will you allow her to sit in the sedan chair, in which she may at least be sheltered from the night? Or would you rather have the baby's death on your conscience?'

The soldier showed no signs of relenting. Robert followed up, 'Sir, the writ has no mention that Huguenots are not permitted to shelter in a sedan chair, has it not?'

'Please, officer,' implored Suzanne, who then approached the soldier and pressed two gold coins into his palm. This had the desired effect. He gave the command to carry the chair a good few blocks from the house, despite Suzanne's insistence that it be deposited at Place des Monges, which was just a stone's throw away at the end of the street.

Jeanne took leave of her sister in their secret satisfaction that the commanding officer had not made any reference to the other children. No one but the soldiers was allowed to accompany her.

Once in the dark street, they did not progress more than ten paces when one of the men put down the sedan chair, provoking the other soldier to do likewise. 'No one told us to carry the bleedin' Hugo, did they?' he said to his counterpart. Then, pulling back the flap, he said to Jeanne: 'You can get out and walk, you lazy bitch!'

Jeanne, without a word and suppressing her fear, climbed out of the chair, which started the baby off.

'Shut your brat up 'n' all before I bash its brains against the wall,' said the other soldier, manifestly proud to go one up on the previous rant.

It was under such harassment that Jeanne walked three paces behind the dragoons across Place des Monges, now dark and secret, through the silent lanes where only cats' eyes shone, and on to the main square, where the uneven cobbles were empty and glistening in the moonlight.

This was where she would spend a sleepless night. But she was nonetheless relieved when her tormentors left the moment they set down the chair. She had been worried that, under the influence of their perverse diversion, their threats might spill into action just to goad each other on. Instead, while pursuing their conversation about the lack of proper whores in Montauban, they marched back the way they had come. It was already a quarter to the hour, and soldiers were not permitted out after nine o'clock. Moreover, all street lighting would soon be extinguished.

Jeanne now sat inside the sedan chair, gave her baby her breast, and prayed in the darkness, thanking God for their deliverance.

8

28 August to September 1685

THE COLD PALE light of early morning brought with it the smell of fresh bread from a nearby bakery.

Alone in the sedan chair on the market square, Jeanne woke from her intermittent sleep. Slowly, she eased herself into a different position, her thoughts turning again to the looming shame of being on public display. Especially since below the chair, a puddle on the cobbles, tainted with blood, still betrayed an unavoidable call of nature.

The creak and slap of wooden shutters being pushed open, and secured against the brick facades of upstairs apartments, announced the imminent opening of the gallery shops that surrounded the royal square. And soon, the first market sellers would be carting in their produce and poultry from the country.

But she was not alone, she kept telling herself. She knew from experience that there are a great many horrid storms in life to bear up to, which, once overcome, inevitably lead to more clement days. Besides, she had her beautiful baby, whose warmth and smell was better than bread, and she had God.

No, she was not alone, but she would still have to make a move before the bells chimed six o'clock, when shoppers would start pouring onto the square. Where would she go, though? Place des Monges? The stone bench of her childhood was still there on the west side of the square; it had the advantage of receiving the sun's warmth at the start of the day. She remembered travelling in the post office coach as a young girl and it hitting a bollard there and damaging a wheel. She had huddled with her sister on that bench, grateful for the pool of early- morning sunlight, until help had been sent for and the wheel repaired. What would that little girl have thought at seeing herself now on that same stone bench, a lone woman with a baby in search of warmth?

But she was not alone, she kept telling herself as the neighing, mooing, and clucking of animals and the chattering of country folk grew louder outside her modest wooden refuge. Again she prayed to God to give her strength to leave it before the crowds began to gather, before inquisitive heads started to peep in through the curtain. But after a sleepless, unclean night, she simply could not muster the courage to take the first, degrading step out. She could not face the shame.

Suddenly the flap was pulled aside, letting in a stream of light.

'Oh, my God!' said a man's voice. 'What in God's name have they done?'

Jeanne looked up through silent tears. Monsieur Picquos, the draper, discreetly closed the flap and said, 'Madame Delpech, please, forgive me, I had no idea you would be inside. I sent word to Madame, your sister, thinking the chair had been stolen. She has sent Antoine here.'

He called out to David, his lackey, then said to Jeanne, 'I fear I cannot take you in, but do not worry, Madame Delpech. Antoine knows where to take you. David will help carry you there.'

Jeanne had by now calmed her emotions. 'Thank you, Monsieur, you are most kind,' she said as the sedan chair was lifted. A splash of water chased away the bloody residue left behind her.

'Madame,' said Antoine after a few moments, 'I have been instructed to take you to Place des Monges. Once the guards have left the house, Monsieur Garrisson will come to collect you.'

*

Elizabeth loved being at Aunt Suzanne's. Aunt Suzanne treated her like a proper lady. Elizabeth liked to speak to her about all the things that passed through her mind, especially since her little sister Lulu had taken up more and more of her mother's time, and now there was the baby to contend with.

'Why can we not be like everyone else?' she said to her aunt on the morning after her mother had been taken away. She was perched, prim and proper, on the large bed the children had shared in the third-floor bedroom. The curtains had been drawn back from around it, and grey morning light filled the room. 'Lots of my friends have become Catholics, and they are still the same as before. I mean, they have not grown boils on their faces or grown devil's horns or become mad or anything, except for mad Rose, but she was already mad, deaf and dumb, and now she is gone to the nunnery anyway.'

'It is a question of faith, my darling,' said her aunt as she finished dressing Lulu in her son Pierre's murrey robe. 'Your faith is your most precious gift from God. It is what carries your immortal soul to heaven when you die. If you lose it, then so, too, will your soul be lost.'

'But Uncle Robert has forsaken the religion,' said Elizabeth.

'No, my dear, you must never say that,' said Suzanne, a little taken aback. 'He signed a piece of paper; that is all.' Her voice then wavered with an emotion that contrasted with her natural cheeriness when she said, 'It is true, though, he has resolved to make a sacrifice to keep all of us out of harm's reach, even though I fear it will prey heavy on his soul. But it may well be that God has chosen your uncle so that he may help your mama.'

Suzanne, having finished dressing Louise, clapped her hands to get everyone's attention and said, 'Come now, children, remember the plan.'

'I'd much rather stay here, my aunt,' said Elizabeth. 'Travelling makes me feel awfully sick at the best of times.'

'No buts, Lizzy, my dear, you know your mother needs you. Remember, you must hide in . . .?'

'The horrible trunk!' said Elizabeth.

'Yes. Only until you get through the gate. Your mother will give you the baby to look after while she takes Lulu on her knees.'

'Why can't Paul go in the trunk and me under the blanket?'

'Your brother cannot be expected to look after a baby, now, can he, darling angel?'

Lulu tottered over to her big sister. Elizabeth picked her

up like a proper little mother, then turned her round, sinking her face into the crook of the child's neck.

'Lulu, you look like a boy. Are you a boy, Lulu?' she said to the child with a laugh.

'Not boy, no,' said the toddler pouting.

'You look splendid, my Lulu,' said Suzanne. 'Lizzy is only teasing; do not take any notice of her,' she said, frowning at Elizabeth to indicate she should be more compliant.

'I was only playing, Lulu. You look splendid.'

'Spendid,' said little Pierre to his cousin. He and Lulu were the same age, give or take a month. It was a good job he was not yet breeched; otherwise Louise really would have looked like a boy.

'Let me put on your hat for you,' said Aunt Suzanne, catching the child's head with a bonnet that had a sausage of cloth around it for protection against bumps. 'There,' she said as she attached it beneath her niece's chin. 'Now, Lulu, if you really love Pierre, you will be glad to wear his clothes for a while, just for a while. You do love him, don't you?'

Lulu responded by scrambling down from the high mattress, jumping off the bed step, and giving chase to her cousin with lips puckered. Everyone laughed, even Paul, who was slumped in the armchair. He had been down in the mouth without his mother.

Suzanne had to tell them to hush for fear of alerting the guards three floors below at the *porte cochère*. Then she clapped her hands again and gave the three children one last rundown of what they must do: stay hidden in the coach either inside the trunk or under the blanket, except for Lulu, who would sit on her mother's lap and say nothing.

'But what if the baby cries?' said Elizabeth.

'It is a risk, but we shall get word to your mama to make sure baby has had her fill before going through the gate.'

Elizabeth knew exactly what her aunt meant; she had seen her mother giving her breast before. She wondered how long it would take for her breasts to grow. She hoped to God they would not be as small as Anette's.

'That way she will be contented and sleep through,' said Suzanne.

They heard steps on the landing. Pierre instinctively ran to his mother, Lulu to her sister. Then the door was pushed open.

'They are gone at last,' said Robert. He looked haggard, but managed a bright smile at the children. Turning back to his wife, he said, 'I gave them my word Jeanne would not come back and a louis d'or to each so they would leave us in peace early.'

He read love and gratitude in his wife's eyes that needed no words. He took the hands she and Pierre held out to him as she said, 'You'd better get going, Robert, before it gets too hot on the road. With the help of the Lord, you will be there by lunchtime. I only hope your back bears up and that dear Jeanne will be able to endure the bone-shaking.'

'Last week's rain will have moistened the ground. The road will not be quite so hard. I just hope we make it through the gate.'

*

It was approaching eight o'clock when a coach, drawn by a magnificent pair of horses, stopped at Montmurat gate, east of the town.

It contained a lawyer, his wife, and a little boy wearing a

pudding hat and not yet in breeches, and was driven by a valet. Robert pulled down the window and told the guard he was taking his spouse and son to his country house. His eyes then stared in dismay before he quickly regained his composure; he had recognised one of the soldiers, who had been quartered at his house before his conversion. The soldier approached the lawyer's carriage which he fleetingly admired before looking inside.

'I know him,' he said, then glared at the woman and the child. Suzanne and Jeanne were from the same mould; apart from their age, it would be difficult to tell them apart in broad daylight, let alone in the shadows of a bourgeois carriage. The children did not cough; the baby did not cry. After a moment's pause which seemed to last an eternity, the guard said: 'A new Catholic, he can pass.'

It was all Jeanne could do to keep from fainting, such was the flush of relief. 'Thank God,' she sighed as they rolled into the Bordeaux road that followed the river Tarn, glorious and luxuriant at this time of year. But Jeanne's thoughts were already elsewhere: they were with Jacob.

*

The Marquis de Boufflers was exquisitely dressed as always. His blue damask just-au-corps with gold trim reflected his high spirits. And his beautifully flowing periwig quivered dashingly whenever he moved his head.

He was having luncheon at the bishop's palace and enjoying the chance to relate the news again of the king's jubilation over the miraculous abjurations. The nation was no longer plagued by a state within a state, and Louis could reign proudly over a kingdom united in one faith. Both the bishop and the intendant solemnly agreed, reintegrating those who had been deprived of their Roman Catholic heritage for so long had made the kingdom whole again. They had at last found the right method, harsh but not violent. More humane and less costly than bloodletting, the dragonnades were the way to go.

For the bishop, the conversions constituted the summit of years of relentless hard work, repairing the spiritual foundations of the city. He had not only carried out missionary forays throughout the diocese, but governed the construction of the Hotel Dieu Hospital, the episcopal palace, and the Jesuit College.

He was filled with inner satisfaction that his labours had so pleased His Majesty, not to mention Rome, where the conversions of Montauban were the talk of the Quirinal Palace. He could not have prayed for a better reward. Now, to cap it all, he just needed a proper seat for his diocese brimming with new converts. He needed a cathedral.

'I should strike while the iron is hot,' said de Boufflers, sitting on the opposite side of the great oaken table, 'while the king is still under the exultation of having a thorn removed from his royal side!'

'Actually,' said the bishop, feeling his chin, 'I was thinking of asking the question as soon as that abject edict is fully nullified. There is hardly a Huguenot in the kingdom, so it should not take long, should it?'

'Now that the best part of the reformists has embraced the true faith, you can be sure the wording is being finalised as we speak,' said de Boufflers, who dabbed the corners of his mouth before drawing from his glass.

'If I had any say in the matter,' said intendant le Goux de

La Berchère from the end of the table, 'I should have it built not in brick, but in stone.' He paused for two beats for those present to seize the full measure of his statement. Everyone knew that churches in Montauban were traditionally built of brick, which was the natural building resource of the generality. It was what gave the town and surrounding villages their cheerful peachy hue. The intendant continued: 'It would stand as a statement of royal power.'

'Indeed,' said the bishop fervently, brandishing a chicken wing, 'and a reminder of Catholic prevalence over the Protestant congregation, now defunct!'

'Defunct but not quite eradicated,' said the intendant. 'Alas, there are still a few recalcitrant bourgeois who think themselves above the rest. Honestly, they are a thorn in *my* side: they are spoiling my conversion rate!'

'Hmm, quite a predicament, I dare say,' said the marquis with a quiver of the periwig. 'The rabble, one can easily dispose of, but the bourgeois are a bit awkward, I must admit.'

Between two bites of chicken, the bishop said: 'It is such a shame, especially when everything else is going so well.'

'Would you believe,' said the intendant, 'that Delpech fellow had the audacity to come knocking at my door, complaining of ill treatment? Honestly, is the man completely naive?'

'What did you say?' asked de Boufflers, sucking a quail leg bone.

'I ordered him to regain his house to receive another eight soldiers,' said the intendant. Then, delicately raising a long finger, he added: 'And their horses!'

'Hah. Outrageous!' said the marquis, who burst out in an

extravagant laugh, making his wig tremble.

'I then had a notice pinned to his door, stating that soldiers will find food and lodging at this inn.'

'Ho, ho, ingenious!'

'Not really; the philistine still won't see reason. He is becoming a perfect pest. Not only does he have nothing left to sell for the subsistence of his guests, I fear he is in danger of becoming a dissenter, or worse, a martyr.'

'We can't have that,' said the bishop, nearly choking on a morsel of chicken.

'I know what,' said the marquis, with the nonchalant flourish of another quail leg. 'We'll send him to prison for a spell. That should knock the stuffing out of him.'

'Yes, and I'll have everyone say prayers to facilitate his return to the fold.' The bishop gave a bovine-eyed glance to the marble Virgin Mary on the mantle, and then held out his glass for more of the excellent 'blood' of Christ.

'That might do the trick,' said the intendant, rubbing the stubble on his chin. 'It cannot hurt; at the very least, it will send out a strong message to those thinking of converting back.'

'And what about the man's wife?' said de Boufflers.

'We let her go. She is staying at one of her brother-in-law's farms near Villemade with her children. At least, this way, she is out of sight and out of mind.'

'Quite,' said the bishop. 'There is nothing worse than a mother and infant to soften public opinion.'

'But I shall deal with her once her baby is weaned,' said the intendant.

Taking up his glass, the marquis said: 'I give you the king, the church, and our continued success!'

'Amen,' said the bishop.

9

November 1685 to April 1686

JEANNE WAS SITTING on a three-legged stool, tossing a long-handled copper chestnut pan over the kitchen fire.

The maid had gone to milk the goat. Lizzy, Lulu, and Paul were chasing hens in the farmyard. The baby, having been given the breast, gurgled contently in her cot. It struck Jeanne that the cries and cackles outside were louder now that the surrounding trees had dropped their leaves with the first frost.

The resonant rasping of jays in the oak thicket roused her from her fire-gazing. The children's cries then ceased; she turned to the window that looked over the farmyard. A squat man was walking away down the earthen track; it could only be the weaver from the cottage near the river. Paul and his sisters were running back to the farmhouse.

A moment later, pushing open the stiff door, the boy said, 'Mama, a letter for you.'

'It must be from Papa,' said Elizabeth, holding Lulu against her hip.

Jeanne handed the chestnut pan handle to Paul and took the folded paper. She stepped into the light of the south-facing window by the solid stone sink. Then, hastily, she broke the seal, unfolded the letter, and read to herself.

'*My dear wife,*

'*Once the soldiers had sold all the livestock of our farms, I was escorted here to the Château Royal one morning by the marshal, Monsieur Castagne, and three archers. The marshal gave orders that I am to see no one, but rest assured, I am not alone in this otherwise dark and forlorn cell. I am with our Lord, and every day, I give praise to Him for shedding His light on my poor existence. As you have time and again reminded me during our previous hardships, we are nothing without God. My dear wife, without His hope and love, there can be no rightfulness, no morals, no conscience.*

'*I have been told unendingly by the guards that I am to be hanged or sent to America. But abjure, I will not. On the contrary, such barbarism only strengthens my spirit and determination to follow my conscience. I am resolved to die rather than be my own betrayer. Indeed, I am filled with a deep joy that every day, God gives me strength I never thought I had, and helps me get through all sorts of ordeals.*

'*One of the guards, the one to whose heart God sent pity and who brought this quill with which I write, tells me I am to be transferred to the prison of Cahors, where prisoners are assembled to join a convoy to the galley ships at Marseille. Even if I am condemned to the life of a galley slave, I will not abjure.*

'*If you could get some straw to me, at least I will have bedding, and a quilt would be most welcome during these cold months. But, my love, you must stay away yourself and try to find a passage out of the realm as soon as the warmer weather comes. I only hope and pray our children will bear up to the long journey. I have left instructions with Robert concerning my affairs, our home, and Verlhac, though I wonder if we shall ever see them again.*

'You can imagine that I would like with all my heart to see you before my imminent transfer, but please stay away, my love. It pains me truly to say I fear our next rendezvous may well be in heaven. I wish you many blessings, my dear, beloved wife.'

Jeanne closed her eyes. She needed to empty her mind so that she would not be overwhelmed by emotion when she explained to her children that their father was in prison, but alive and well.

*

Robert Garrisson knew that signing the abjuration certificate and receiving the bishop's absolution would not suffice.

New Catholics were expected to make an appearance at Sunday Mass. This in turn meant partaking in the Holy Communion—which, for a Protestant, was like asking a Saracen to eat pork—or risk being considered a bad Catholic. Robert knew what that meant.

Being a bad Catholic brought with it the same punishment as being a Huguenot fugitive trying to leave the country. Garrisson knew if he did not play along, it could mean being condemned to a life on a galley ship, and his status and fortune would make no difference at all, and neither would his age. He had seen young men and old, the labourer and the master, the merchant and the thief, indiscriminately sent to the galleys, some for three years, others for ten, some never to return.

Posing as a good Catholic, on the other hand, brought exoneration of taxes for the year past, the right to continue his law practice, and to retain his houses, farms, and fortune.

To a man approaching seventy, this was nonetheless little reward compared to the ruin of his soul. Robert at times felt miserable and increasingly weighed down with guilt over his conversion.

One day, sensing her husband beginning to withdraw into himself, Suzanne said, 'Once you have helped Jacob and Jeanne out of the country, we shall join them and live our faith in peace.'

It was delivered with such mirth and simplicity, and Robert did appreciate his wife's thoughtfulness. But he knew deep down that starting a new life in another country at his age, even if he could get over the border as a Catholic, would be infinitely difficult. Besides, now that he had a son, his family name would survive despite the present crisis.

So he resolved to try to live with his conscience. He would defend Jacob and watch over Jeanne, not to mention his dear wife. She had not abjured. His conversion as the chief of the household had sufficed to rid his house of the dragoons. Nobody had yet said anything against her. As long as she did not overtly proclaim her faith or partake in any clandestine Protestant gathering, she would be able to withstand the hostile climate until reason prevailed again in France, he thought. By that time, he might no longer be part of this world, but the satisfaction of safeguarding her person and soul and those of his descendants gave a sense to his life which always cheered him up. And what if God had meant for him to be an instrument of His grace to help his fellows? Then should he not rather rejoice?

Robert knew he was walking on thin ice by taking on the defence of his friend and brother-in-law. Jacob Delpech was not only determined to stick to his faith, but had resolved to plead his innocence against whatever motive it was that had put him in jail.

The soldier's prediction of Jacob's imminent transfer turned out to be wrong, no doubt partly due to the impracticalities of travelling in harsh weather. The earth roads would be deeply rutted, and getting stuck in the Causses du Quercy on the way to Cahors could mean dying of cold or hunger.

Delpech had nonetheless managed to win the trust of the youngest of the guards. His name was Francis, an average-sized man with bovine eyes who confessed to thinking as little as possible about God.

One day, through the bars of his cell, Jacob said to the soldier, 'You do realise you are going to die?'

The soldier quipped that at least he wouldn't have to endure the 'excitement' of a life standing in front of prison cells anymore.

'But then what?' said Jacob. 'Where will your soul go?'

'Don't know, don't care. Besides, heaven's a place for bourgeois and priests, far as I'm concerned.'

'You are wrong, my good man. Eternal life is promised to all those who persevere in God's love until the end.'

The soldier knew what God's love meant for some priests, but he kept it to himself. Instead, he just let the bourgeois rattle on about how anyone could save their soul, be they born in the Château de Versailles or the *cour des miracles*. At least it passed the time of day, and made a change from thinking about what he would do once he had saved up enough coin to get a wife. He had his eye on the fruit and veg seller's third daughter. She might be boss-eyed, but she had a fair-enough nature, wide mothering hips, and a generous pair of jugs.

Since that day, conversations between Francis and Jacob had been discreet and few, but there had been enough of them to sow seeds of faith where once the soldier's soul had been a barren field. After all, what if all that God stuff really was true? So the soldier thereafter agreed to pass correspondence to and from Robert, in exchange for a fee for the risk taken.

*

Throughout his detention in Montauban, only once did Jacob sway.

He was sharing his cell with a new inmate, a certain Monsieur Edmond Galet, a loquacious tailor. Galet had been caught trying to reach Bordeaux via the post boat that ran from Toulouse via Agen. On the boat, he had entered into cordial conversation with a young, well-spoken gentleman named Boisset. To distinguish himself from the rabble of labourers, Edmond became congenial with the younger man to the point of inadvertently giving away one or two details of his and his wife's intentions, which were to go on a trip to London. It turned out that the young man had nothing to his name but the clothes on his back and the title of third son to a lesser lord near Toulouse. Seizing the occasion, he informed the authorities the moment the boat moored in Agen to let the passengers get some refreshment. Edmond Galet was questioned and arrested; his wife abjured. In accordance with the king's declaration of August 1685, Boisset was able to walk away with half of the value of Galet's wealth as reward for the denunciation.

Monsieur Galet could no longer suffer the vermin, the insalubrity, and the dampness of winter. Through teeth chattering with cold, he told Jacob his plan.

'I will sign this confounded paper if it will free me of this intolerable dungeon,' he said in whispers, so that the other prisoners, mostly common villains and thugs, could not hear and thus denounce him in exchange for a reduced sentence.

'Abjure?' said Jacob in a voice equally low.

'Abjure, no, or if that is what it is, then I will do it only for the time it takes for me to leave the country. For my plan is to escape to Brandenburg, where I have heard that Huguenots are welcome to practice their employ and religion freely. You should think about it, Monsieur Delpech.'

'I cannot forsake my faith, not even for ten minutes,' said Jacob. 'I cannot become that imposture.'

'Life, is it not a game of charades? Do you not play a role when you are buying and selling? When you want to seduce your wife? And you do not act the same to a lowly pauper as to a lordly buyer, do you not?'

'Not I,' said Jacob. 'And I believe it has been the reason for my past success. My produce is guaranteed, and my word is good. My clients know that they will not be deceived.'

'Suit yourself. But if you dig in your heels like a donkey does its hooves, then I fear the future bodes not well for you, my friend.'

Shortly after their conversation, Monsieur Galet was released from the abominable prison. On handing Jacob his sack of straw, the tailor whispered, 'It pains me to leave you, good Sir. But I would argue that the Lord gave me the inspiration, and I have chosen not to be shy of his grace. Think on it.'

Monsieur Galet left the dismal dungeon and, from what Jacob could gather, he lost no time in carrying out his project.

The conversation left Delpech torn between two minds for the next week, the first penetratingly cold week of winter. Could signing the declaration really be a means sent by God to help the faithful to pastures new? But despite all the toing and froing in his mind, Jacob also knew that he himself constituted, as did the first martyrs, an example to his fellows. If he abjured, then any moral resistance would end in the hearts of his fellow co-religionists. And his self-esteem and credibility, even if he recovered his faith elsewhere, would be shattered. He knew he represented something greater than himself now: he had become a moral touchstone. He could not convert; he could not betray God or himself for a single minute.

*

Robert had found an angle of attack, even though he still did not know on what legal grounds Jacob had been incarcerated. He had built up a defence based on the very edict of October that had revoked and replaced the Edict of Nantes. Article XII of the Edict of Fontainebleau gave a glimmer of hope to Jeanne and Jacob because it clearly stated that '*liberty is granted to persons of the so-called Reformed Religion, pending the time when it shall please God to enlighten them as well as others, to remain in the cities and places of our kingdom, lands, and territories subject to us, and there to continue their commerce, and to enjoy their possessions, without being subjected to molestation or hindrance on account of the so-called Reformed Religion.*'

Robert had tried to use his influence and relations to find out if and when Jacob would stand before the judges. Each time he addressed the consuls, he was fobbed off with some excuse about the backlog of judicial cases due to the new context brought about by the Edict of October. In short, Jacob could very well be left to rot as far as the authorities were concerned.

Robert reformulated letter after letter to the intendant during the winter months to reiterate his concerns and to try to extract answers. He knew full well he was in danger of becoming a nuisance.

In January, a close source to de la Berchère who had known Robert for forty years advised him to ease off for a while, or risk causing a calamity for Delpech's family, not to mention his own. He told Robert he would receive an answer in due course.

*

Late February, there was already a feeling of spring in the air. The exceptional weather over the past few days now induced the first daffodils on the esplanade to unravel their yellow heads under the plane trees. Windows throughout the city had been flung open to let in the clean, warm air.

Robert was in good spirits. He was at his desk, writing another note to Jacob. The intendant had at last informed him he would receive knowledge of Jacob's charge very soon. This meant Garrisson could shortly begin Jacob's defence and challenge his detention. Robert was dripping hot wax onto the note when there was a loud knock at the front door.

Antoine entered the downstairs study and handed his master a note with no seal. It was from Robert's town hall contact. Robert read: '*Transfer to Cahors planned for Wednesday, by lettre de cachet.*'

He had to sit down before his legs failed him. It was a

double blow. Jacob's transfer to Cahors would create jurisdiction and coordination difficulties, but worst of all, the order had been given through a lettre de cachet.

A lettre de cachet with the king's seal enforced judgements that could not be appealed, the king being above the law. Robert knew well how easily it had been used as a tool to mute so-called agitators, and even disobliging wives. He remembered the case of one man who, having converted several years earlier, had demanded that a lettre de cachet be made out for his wife in order to shut her up once and for all in a convent, so she could be 'instructed' in the Catholic religion.

In short, all of Garrisson's efforts in building a case for Jacob's defence were dashed. He would be sentenced without a trial. Robert scribbled another note which he arranged to be sent to Jeanne.

*

Towards the end of March, the wind of Autan blew for six days solid, enough to drive anyone insane.

It could blow so hard that one's face grew numb, then drop to a whisper, before cunningly whisking up again. It kept townsfolk cloistered with fear of falling tiles, and farmhands busy with fallen trees. Not far from Villemade, a tall lime tree had cracked at midpoint, and the top part had gone crashing onto the roof of a barn.

Jeanne's maid, Marie, was milking the goat at the time. The animal had obstinately shifted to the opposite end, out of the draft and away from the rattling bar of the barn door. With an appalling crack, a cluster of tiles smashed to the ground where she usually pulled up her milking stool.

Jeanne dashed out of the house fearing the worst, but the girl stood up on the other side of the rubble, unscathed. The goat's move had saved her life. It was one of those moments that made Jeanne reflect on the fragility of life on earth compared to the eternity of heaven.

April was the gambolling season. The grass was now lush and plentiful, and the spring lambs would soon be weaned from their mothers. Jeanne's baby, a happy, gurgling child, was already sitting up on her own and chewing on a quignon of bread.

Now that the baby no longer needed breastfeeding, Jeanne was able to dedicate more time to her other children's education. Just because they had fallen upon hard times, that did not mean their spiritual and academic instruction should be neglected. Elizabeth and Paul could be taught together. Lulu required more attention, especially since Jeanne had been half-amused, half-horrified to hear her utter words in patois. This was due to the influence of Marie, who was more fluent in the local dialect than in the national language.

Even though she had fallen to living beneath herself, Jeanne was well aware that it was breeding and instruction that distinguished one class from another. She was determined that her children would retain the bourgeois values in hand with the religious doctrine taught by Calvin.

It had always been an ancestral satisfaction that her family had been in the law or in the cloth. Her grandfather had been a second consul of Montauban and member of the now-abolished Huguenot consistory, whose job it was to oversee people's moral attitudes and behaviour. Oh, if he could see them now, she often thought.

There had been whispers and fears that the new Catholics

would revert to their former religion and rise up against state repression, drawing in surrounding support of Protestant countries into another bloody war of religion. Jeanne did not want war, no more so than anyone else. There had been enough horrid tales of butchery from the last century which were still within living memory from when she was a child.

But the king had been clever enough to make the Edict of Fontainebleau appear to state that Protestants were still tolerated in France, and their rights to property protected. Surrounding states would thus not be officially offended, and their heads of state would be able to save face against their detractors. What was more, England now had a Catholic king.

April was also the time for a good spring cleaning and to beat out the bedbugs. Jeanne had kept them at bay through the winter by dabbing wine vinegar onto the skin of her children. But of late, Paul had developed a rash.

Now that she had recovered her figure, Jeanne was sprightly as ever. With the help of Marie, she had managed to wash all the bed linen in vinegar and lavender, and then leave it out to dry and to bleach before the sun turned cold. Despite the fatigue of the long day's work, she felt an appeasement within that she had not experienced since before the soldiers rapped on her door in Rue de la Serre. The farmhouse felt much nicer, and the children's clothes that her sister had managed to retrieve were neatly folded away, in anticipation of the change of season.

Jeanne sat at the kitchen table opposite the south-facing window. It looked onto the little courtyard and barn, where Marie and the children were rounding up the chickens into their pen. Nowadays, she much preferred to write in the light of day, and in less than an hour, it would be dark.

Glancing out of the window had become a habit now that Lulu was more often outside than in. Jeanne always directed her eyes first at the water well which she had warned Lizzy and Paul time again not to let Lulu go near. Reassured to see the girls together chasing the last chickens, she fell back to perusing her short account of life on the farm. She knew it would bolster her husband to know they at least were well. It would also soften the blow of her sister's abjuration, she thought, as again she dipped her quill in the oak gall ink.

Suzanne had recently announced her conversion in a letter in which she also related her inner turmoil. The growing fear of a Protestant revolt had led the authorities to increase their vigilance towards new Catholic households. The penalty for clandestine meetings or even being caught reading from a reformist Bible was severe. One such case had recently come to light at a chateau where both lord and male servants were given life on a galley ship, and the ladies and maids a life sentence in prison. The poor children were sent to convents, the rich to be raised by Catholic foster parents using the proceeds of the sale of their parents' properties, the best part of which went to the royal treasury.

Fearing for his wife, his son, and his heritage, Robert had given Suzanne an ultimatum. Either she would have to sign the abjuration certificate, or she would have to leave the country as soon as possible. Papers could be obtained, but if caught at the frontier, the penalty would be no less than life. Suzanne chose to stand by her husband.

The worst was when she had been obliged to perform what the authorities termed as the Easter duty, which meant taking the sacrament. Was it not an insult to Christ to read in the scriptures of the necessity of such superfluous rituals when what was really taught was love and faith?

Jeanne looked up again from her writing. She immediately noticed a hen strutting proudly along the ledge of the well, and Lizzy and Paul with Marie. But where was Lulu? She pushed away the wooden stool from under her and called out through the open window.

'Lizzy, Marie. Where's Lulu?'

Immediately, everyone started searching and calling out. Marie ran to the well. But before Jeanne could reach the back door, a patting on the other side of it brought her instant relief. Jeanne opened the door, scooped up her young daughter, embraced her, and said, 'Louise, there you are, my little angel. Go see Lizzy, darling.'

From the doorsill, she stepped into view of the others near the barn. 'Found her!' she sang out. And to her eldest daughter, she said, 'Lizzy, I told you not to let her out of your sight; you know how fast she can run now.'

'But I boarded over the well, Mother,' said Paul in defence. It wasn't the first time Lulu's disappearance had sent them all into a panic.

'Never mind, do as I say, please, children. Keep together at all times: you must always stay together. Now, I must finish my letter to your father.'

'Yes, Mother,' said Paul and Elizabeth.

'Come on, Lulu, come and feed the *conilhs*,' said Marie, using the patois for *rabbits*.

*

After supper, with the children asleep in the room next door, the maid ironed the last of the fresh linen. While making up a parcel for her husband, Jeanne tried out some patois on Marie. It was an amusement to them both.

Marie had been in awe when Jeanne first arrived at the farm, not knowing what to expect from such a lady. But awe quickly turned to admiration on witnessing how Jeanne retained her dignity in adversity, despite having fallen so low.

The maid, a plain-thinking, plain-faced girl of twenty, no longer regretted not leaving the farm with the previous tenants, a Huguenot farmer and his wife, who had fled to Geneva, the previous spring to keep their religion. It was not often that a peasant girl could observe the ways of a lady so closely. Despite her abjuration, Marie's Protestant faith was stronger than ever, and the frequent evening readings of the Bible with Jeanne comforted her. It was satisfying that, despite their condition, God's law had the same resonance with them both. In this, they were equal.

It had even bemused the girl to see Jeanne getting her hands into the washing, though she would not allow her to fetch the water, nor the milk; it simply was not right and did not respect the established order of things. A lady of quality could not pretend to be a peasant or vice versa. Nevertheless, Jeanne's attempt at speaking words in patois really did make her laugh out loud like a donkey.

'What is the word for *acorn?*' said Jeanne, smiling at the acorn faces that Paul had made for the parcel. Each acorn had been carefully selected from big to small to represent a member of their family. There were six of them.

'*Aglan,*' said Marie.

Jeanne repeated the word and added the happy acorns to the writing material contained in a wooden case, along with a blanket, the previous one having been stolen.

The peasants and crofters in the surrounding farmsteads who had taken on the cultivation of Robert's fields were mostly converted Huguenots. But like Marie, they were Huguenots to the core all the same. Despite some marginal jealousy, Jeanne was nonetheless mostly among people of her faith.

Some of them offered her produce from their winter store. Spontaneous generosity? Or was it to appease their own mortal souls for their lack of resistance? Jeanne neither condemned nor condoned. Some wanted to justify their abjuration, but nobody could look her in the eye and explain they had converted through fear of losing their livelihood, their heritage, their children, when she, a well-born lady, had already given up so much more.

Whatever their reasons, Jeanne accepted their produce as a manifestation of God's grace, though she always insisted on paying. No, she would not accept charity so easily. It would be like profiteering on poor souls in turmoil, and besides, there may come a time when she would truly need it.

Jeanne slipped her letter inside the parcel, which she fastened with some string for it to be ready when the weaver arrived.

Monsieur Cordelle, who was in his mid-thirties, travelled to Cahors once every few weeks to sell his cloth at the market, there being fewer weavers in Cahors than in and around Montauban, where the famous *cadis* and the *gros* de Montauban were produced.

A specific rap at the door announced the weaver. He deliberately used the same codified knock every time he came, and the maid opened the door without a second thought. She had to suppress a scream, however, when she saw not the squat, jovial figure of Monsieur Cordelle, but a tall, stooping frame that filled the doorway. Noticing the weaver standing behind, she then realised it was Monsieur Robert Garrisson, the owner whom she had seen close-up only a few times during her life at the farm.

'Robert! What is it?' said Jeanne as he doffed his hat and walked into the room. Cordelle followed behind. With Robert's presence, Jeanne noticed that the chairs and the table, indeed the entire room, suddenly looked drab and confined. She dared not think how she must look; probably like a farmer's wife.

'I came as soon as I could.'

'It is Suzanne, isn't it?'

'No, dear Jeanne, it is not Suzanne,' said Robert in earnest. 'I have come to save you from prison. They are coming here at first light to arrest you and take the children.'

He was relieved to get it out quickly; there was no point in beating about the bush. But he had been wondering how he would tell her since his contact at the town hall gave him the information that very afternoon. He was relieved, too, that the flash of alarm that darted through her eyes immediately turned to steely determination.

'They cannot!'

'Alas, they can, Jeanne,' said Robert. He wanted to console her in his arms, but his upbringing forbade it. He continued compassionately. 'They can, since the decree of January which states that children under sixteen are to be brought up as Catholics, which means removing them from their Huguenot parents. I am so sorry, Jeanne. I am powerless.'

Powerless. The syllables hammered through her brain and seemed to flatten all hope. She brought her hands together in prayer, but her knees buckled beneath her. Robert and Monsieur Cordelle were able to catch hold of her in time and ease her into the spindle-back chair by the oak trestle table.

'Poor, poor woman,' said Monsieur Cordelle. ''Tis too much for her to bear. I don't know how she's managed to take so many setbacks.'

'Because she's a saint woman, Monsieur,' said Marie, who then brought her lady round by dabbing salt and vinegar on her cheeks.

After a moment, Robert spoke. 'Jeanne, my dear Jeanne, you must leave. You must let Monsieur Cordelle take you to safety, or they will lock you up in prison.'

'My children, my babies,' said Jeanne, muffling her outburst with her hand so she did not wake up her children.

'I promise I will arrange to take them into my care. Suzanne will look after them until we can get them to you.'

'You are a good man, Robert, but you also promised to free Jacob. He is still in that foul dungeon after five months of captivity. I know it is beyond your control . . . but, no, I cannot leave my children. Please, do not ask that of me . . .'

'Listen, dear Jeanne, here is a letter from your sister. Suzanne and I already spoke about this eventuality when the decree was published last January. As a new Catholic, I will have the power to take them under my wing. We have both taken the Easter sacrament. There is no reason for the priest to put us on his list of bad Catholics.'

'Don't tell me that is why Suzanne abjured.'

'No, not only. But she knew you would not. And there

were other reasons I imposed, too, I confess.'

Jeanne clasped her hands and closed her eyes. She said, 'I will take them with me away from here.'

'They will never survive the journey,' said Robert, 'not on the run.'

'And what with the lambing season well underway,' said Cordelle, 'the wolves are hungrier than ever—they smell blood. You'd need a good guide.'

Robert knew about the human mind; he knew the sacrifice Jeanne was capable of for her children's well-being. He said, 'I am sorry I have been unable to prepare you for this calamity; I have only just found out myself. I came immediately. But alas, you cannot help your children in prison, Jeanne, nor Jacob for that matter. You must go into hiding. Please, Jeanne, I know how hard this must be, but it is the only way to spare Lizzy of the convent and Paul of the Jesuits.'

Jeanne held her face in her hands. Robert was right: she could not expect her children to go into hiding, let alone flee into the wilderness. And if she stayed, she would be imprisoned, which would be of no good to anyone.

'They are afraid, Jeanne, that all those who refuse to abjure will stir up Protestant feeling, and cause a revolt. They won't let you stay here any longer.'

At length, Jeanne began to gather a few essential effects.

She had found refuge here in her cosy retreat. From here, she had been able to relieve some of her husband's misery. She felt it must have been a happy home the farmers had made. It smelt and felt wholesome, like freshly baked bread and clean linen and lavender. Why, oh why had this injustice fallen upon their community? Why this persecution when

Catholics and Protestants had lived in peace together, traded together? Except for the odd spurt of aggression from high-blooded students, their lives had been good, the plain was fertile—indeed, there could not be a plain more fertile on God's earth. Why did men have to ruin it all?

She spent the whole night preparing to go. Every time, ten, twenty times perhaps, she was on the verge of leaving when she put down her sack of effects, and went quietly back to the bedroom to kiss her sleeping children: Lizzy, her little lady; Lulu, her sweet precious; Paul, such a responsible little boy; and her youngest, whom she time and again plucked from Marie's arms and cradled through the night. as She went from one child to the next, touching their arms, kissing their foreheads as they slept.

Despite Robert's reassurances, as the night began to grow pale, she still could not bring herself to leave them. It was like having her heart wrenched from her chest.

'We really must go now, Madame Delpech,' said the weaver. The cockerel would soon crow; the soldiers would soon come.

Weighed down with fatigue and heartache, to Robert's relief, at last she passed her baby to the maid, and pulled herself away from the farmhouse.

Robert gave instructions to Marie. He then accompanied Jeanne in Monsieur Cordelle's cart as far as the weaver's cottage, where, to avoid arousing suspicion, he had left his own coach. Robert reiterated his reassurances and rode back to Montauban to prepare a case to take custody of the children.

The sky was already half-lit over the furrowed field bordered with hedging; there was no need for the weaver to take a lamp to lead Jeanne to a small farm building where he sometimes worked. It contained a workshop with a spinning wheel, a loom, a table, and a bed ingeniously flattened upright against the wall. He pulled down the bed and removed the wooden partition behind it. This revealed a recess—containing a stool and a bucket—of about three yards wide and two yards deep.

'I am sorry, Madame Delpech: this is where you will have to stay during the day. No one must see you. No one must suspect you are here. You must only come out at night.'

Jeanne thanked him. She knew he would be tortured and publicly hanged if caught harbouring a Huguenot.

10

August and September 1687

(i)

ON THE EVENING of 25 August, a bedraggled company of prisoners rode their pack donkeys into the fortified Mediterranean city of Aigues-Mortes.

Jacob's hands were blistered from the rough cord of the primitive bridle, and his body ached. His clothes had become three sizes too large, and he could feel his bones with the donkey's every stride. He and the rest of the detainees had ridden without stirrups from Montpellier to the walled city, under the escort of fusiliers on foot and archers on horseback.

At their head rode the subdelegate of the intendant of Languedoc. The fourteen captives, men and women of every age and rank, did not look like criminals at all. In fact, despite their visible signs of fatigue and wear, they resembled the townsfolk who watched them pass, mostly in silence, through the crowded lanes of the newly confirmed papist town. And yet, by law, criminals they were. Guilty of favouring their conscience over the king's divine will.

They were the *resistants*, secretly envied by those who looked on, by those who, for whatever reason, lacked strength of faith to remain Protestant.

'Look at the poor wretches,' said a stocky man with burly forearms, unable to keep his thoughts to himself. He had paused with his handcart at the sight of the procession. The man, whose name was Jean Fleuret, secretly said a prayer asking for forgiveness for his own sins, and to give strength to these righteous convicts.

'Aye, I wager 'tis another load for the great crossing,' said the dapper grey-haired man standing next to him. Jean knew the man to be the haberdasher who twice took to the sea in his younger days, but had long since taken over his father's boutique. The man continued in a reminiscent tone of voice, ''Tis soon the season to be leaving. We used to get to the Canaries by mid-November, then crossed at Christmastide. Best time for avoiding the hurricanes.'

'See what you become, eh?' said a rotund man with a pot belly from good living.

'I ask you, Sir,' said Jean Fleuret, pointing to one convict, 'should we not be prouder riding with that poor fellow there than watching this procession of true faith like they were miscreants?' He doffed his hat respectfully to the ragged Huguenot in question, then wheeled his cart full of carpentry tools alongside the company, a short distance towards his home.

Jacob Delpech endeavoured to remain as dignified as possible to show the onlookers he was not a broken man, for he rode with God. It nevertheless came as no small relief to see, at the end of the lane, a bridge over a moat that led to the round Tour de Constance, an impressive and impenetrable vestige of medieval times, and his new prison.

The massive stone tower, walls six yards thick and thirty yards high, housed two dim vaulted chambers, one on each floor. The prisoners were divided into two groups according to their sex. The women and girls were placed downstairs where only a feeble light entered through the arrow slits, but at least they were out of the still-sweltering evening sun. The men were conducted to the vast room above. In each room, they were welcomed by a dozen or so prisoners who had previously arrived.

The intendant's subdelegate had thoughtfully arranged for the reformists to be handed abjuration certificates before the next leg of their long and perilous voyage, a voyage which would take them to America. A woman with a baby at her breast, and an old peasant woman in clogs who wanted to die on the French mainland, signed their conversions. They were instantly set free, at least in body, for their hearts would be bound in the prison of self-reproach.

Jacob was glad that, by the grace of God, Jeanne had not been made to endure such a soul-destroying place. However, the conversions did not trigger a wave of signatures as the subdelegate had hoped. Instead, despite imminent exile and possible death, one lady broke into a psalm and was joined by the other women.

The well of light that ran through the centre of the building carried the soft voices to the upper chamber. The sweet music could not fail to lift the men's hearts, and Jacob broke into song himself. Other men joined in the psalm until the whole tower, to the indignation of guards and officials, resonated like a cathedral of singing parishioners.

It occurred to Jacob that he, like every one of them there,

may sometimes feel downhearted, but mostly they were happy in themselves in that they had remained faithful to their conscience. They were suffering for the highest reward. They were the *resistants*.

*

Their song could be heard across the walled city and had the power to move many new Catholics to pity and envy.

'We cannot sit here and carry on our work with falseness in our hearts as if we were not affected,' said Jean Fleuret to his wife when the singing started. His voice was stern but searching. 'It's as if we never had a conscience in the first place . . . What god would want such hollow souls in his great kingdom?'

They were seated around a sturdy timber table with their three children—two boys, eight and thirteen, and a girl of eleven—and were halfway through their meal. The windows were wide open, with a mosquito gauze placed in the frame, and the land breeze was a welcome refreshment. But the bread had stayed soft, which meant a storm was brewing. However, if it came, at least it would clear the air, and the southern sun would become more clement than before.

The Fleurets thanked the Lord every day at mealtime for their pleasant climate, their modest two-storey stone dwelling, the bread on the table, and the ham in the larder. But what was the sun or the rain to a man who had sold his soul for life's comforts? Too well had they come to know death and had learnt to accept it as an integral part of their short existence. They had lost three children, two of whom had reached the age of ten.

'I feel like I let mine fly out of me like a butterfly,' said

Madame Fleuret, a robust woman with a natural generosity in her round face and smiling eyes. 'But like a butterfly, it keeps coming back to the same spot; then off it flies again before I can catch it.'

Jean stood up. He strode to the sink, pulled out the gauze above it, and closed the windows. He turned around, and in a grave voice, he said, 'I think you were right, my Ginette; I think we ought to leave. I don't want to look back with remorse at my life when the time comes. I want to trust in the future of His kingdom.' He strode back to his chair and sat down. Gesturing with his large, leathery hands, he said, 'Listen, Gigi, I think I can find work in Geneva. In fact, I'm sure of it. Monsieur Grosjean is doing well, I've heard, and he would need a good carpenter.'

'Jeannot, oh, my Jeannot,' said Ginette, clasping her hands. 'I can feel my butterfly coming back!'

'You mean you don't mind?'

'Don't mind? I've been praying so hard for you to change your mind about staying that I've got blisters on the palms of my hands.'

'Hah,' chuckled Jean Fleuret, 'and I've been praying every night for the Lord's enlightenment, and for you to tell me you wanted to leave!' They laughed together, content in their new resolution.

The family made their secret plans. Then the carpenter said, 'Let us pray for our brothers and sisters in the tower, who endure and set the example for us all of true religious fervour and trust in our Lord. And for them was laid in store the crown of life, which God has promised to those who love Him. Amen.'

Such manifestations of faith as the song of the Tower of

Constance did not create a rebellion, but did cause many to seek exile rather than live the sham of a false Catholic.

*

Jacob had only ever made two return journeys over water.

Once, as a young man to London with his father, who attended medical lectures there, and more recently, for business on the post-boat which carried passengers from Toulouse to Bordeaux. He had detested every moment of the two-day trip along the river Garonne and was sick travelling both there and back. How would he fare on the great seas? Until this day, he dared not even think about it; he had put it all to the back of his mind, instead focusing on prayer, psalms, and thoughts of his wife and children.

While in his dungeon in Cahors the intendant of Montauban had visited him with a blank abjuration certificate and news of his children's removal. Though the intendant had willingly used Delpech as an example to would-be bourgeois *resistants*, Jacob's dispossession and imprisonment had been nonetheless a niggling source of bitterness in the otherwise resounding victory of the state over the so-called Reformed Church. His conversion would be the cherry on the cake.

But prior to the visit, Jacob had already received a message about Jeanne's misfortune. The note had been handed to him by an old woman—the same old woman who brought him articles of need such as a blanket, writing material, and fresh straw, and who had passed him a brazier to warm him on the coldest nights.

He knew at least his children would be in safekeeping with his friend and brother-in-law until it pleased God for him to reunite with them. There was no way he could become a Catholic, no more than he could turn lead into gold. Visiting priests, false converters, and other merchants of virtue had not made him convert; neither would the intendant.

The week after the intendant's visit, Jacob was on his way to Montpellier, then to Aigues-Mortes, and now, two days after his incarceration in the round tower, he was about to embark on a tartan. The small, single-mast ship, rigged with a lateen sail and a jib, was to ferry him and the other prisoners to Marseille.

For the crew, it was a lucrative activity, more constant than fishing, and less dangerous than carrying merchandise across the pirate-infested waters of the Mediterranean Sea. Some of the sailors were indifferently cordial in their behaviour towards the prisoners. Others used them to vent all the bitterness of their existence.

One seasoned seafarer in particular looked forward to these little voyages. He unrestrainedly aimed his witty discourse at the vulnerable prisoners while achieving self-gratification by entertaining his fellows with his endless verve. It began the very minute the captives were placed in the hold, when a young lady, no more than sixteen, had the misfortunate of asking this sailor with a benevolent grin and an epicurean twinkle where they were bound. Then he showed his true colours when, in a melodious southern accent, he said: 'From Marseille to Toulon, me lass, then through the treacherous straits of Gibralter to Cadix. That's if you don't get taken by Algerian pirates. Then it be a true and wondrous seafaring voyage that awaits you, my dear, all the way to the other side of the world. That's if you get through the raging winds they call *hurricane*, that whips up the waves as tall as houses, mark my word!

'Oh, aye, I been and seen with me own eyes, see. And I escaped with me life, I did. Then, if you don't get gobbled up by the great creatures that lurk 'neath the ocean waves, they'll set you down on a desert island so you can think of home. That's if you don't get eaten by the cannibals and the giant insects as big as my hand!' He held out his hands as if clutching pears and burst into a pirate-like chuckle. The girl looked squarely at the sailor with pity, as the crew members standing nearby held their bellies in unashamed laughter.

Neither savages nor creatures worried Jacob as he endeavoured to steady himself with every crack of the ship's timbers. Already the gentle sway was brewing a storm in his belly. No, what really worried him was the appalling feeling of seasickness.

The two days and nights that ensued were, for Jacob, worse than the damp, dark, cold two years he had spent behind bars. Under the mistral wind, the vessel pitched and rolled. While the captain and his crew fought to control the ship in the raging sea, all the captives could do was kneel amid the creaking timbers and pray that they would survive the terrifying battering.

Jacob was not the only one to hold his belly in spasms of vomiting. Nearly all of the prisoners became sick. Anyone who was not ill from the swell, soon became so from the stench of vomit and diarrhoea.

It was a harsh baptism of by the sea for most. But the seaworthy among them gave reassurance that the passage to the Americas in this season was rarely so rough, and that, contrary to what the sailors might say, the Caribbean hurricane season would be over by the time they left Cadix. Jacob gave praise to the Lord for this preparation, which nonetheless had strengthened his courage now that he had been put to the test once.

Two days after leaving Aigues-Mortes, the tartan sailed between the impressive forts of St Jean and St Nicolas, and over the massive defensive chain that assured the protection of the Mediterranean port of Marseille.

(ii)

Throughout her husband's confinement in Cahors, Jeanne remained hidden in her recess near Villemade.

In this way, she could arrange for him to receive items for his rudimentary comfort, and was able time and again to exhort him to perseverance, despite his solitude and estrangement from loved ones.

The proximity to Montauban also meant she could receive regular news of her children, who, after an arduous administrative procedure, were now in the care of her sister and brother-in-law. She missed them terribly, and desperately endeavoured every day to keep their faces vivid in her memory.

But one day—it was a Sunday because Marie was not chatting at her spinning wheel—she could no longer see her baby's face. She could only vaguely recall that first smile when she held her in her arms after her birth, and which had helped her bear up to the terrible circumstance of her persecution. But she could no longer call to mind Isabelle's face.

And what of her other children? Would her face fade from their memory as Isabelle's had slipped from hers? Shut away in her recess, she sobbed with visceral pain and thrust her fist in her mouth to keep herself from wailing out. Anyone wandering near the little mud-brick farm building at that time would have heard muffled animal-like howls, but thankfully, there was no one. And no one expected to find Jeanne Delpech de Castanet anywhere in the country, let alone in the countryside of Montauban.

Once it had been assumed that Jeanne had fled the realm, Cordelle had found a pretext to employ Marie at his workshop, and she often stayed there late into the night so that she could pass on his lessons in weaving to Jeanne.

'*Ô boudiou*, tongues may wag, but at least it keeps their minds off me lady,' she had said to Jeanne one night. 'And besides, the weaver i'n't such a bad catch neither!' They had both laughed.

Marie went to church that Sunday, as she did every Sunday according to the law, more to avoid unwelcome attention than through love of the Roman church. That evening, when she closed the shutters, drew down the bed, and pulled away the panel of the recess, it was a drawn and distraught lady who greeted her, the very opposite of the woman Marie had come to admire. Complaining over one's lot was not in Jeanne's breeding, but Marie's forthright questioning soon brought out what had been preying on her lady's mind.

'Have you ever had a portrait done, Madame?' she said, perched on her spinning chair.

'I have,' said Jeanne, seated on the edge of the bed, 'five years ago. My husband insisted on it for posterity. Family, past, present, and future, means everything to him, you see.'

'And a good job too,' said Marie, who spoke in patois, as

did Jeanne more and more often nowadays—you never knew who might be listening outside in the dark. 'Then they won't forget you if your sister hangs it somewhere they can see it every day, will they?'

Marie's bright idea gave Jeanne new wings and instantly brought the colour back to her cheeks. She took up her seat at the loom for another lesson in threading.

When, the following week, Suzanne received news of Jeanne's anxiety, she managed to retrieve her sister's portrait, which she hung up on the wall at the top of the stairs. Then she came up with her own idea that would help bring Jeanne's children back to her, at least in thought. Robert immediately took it up and commissioned an artist to make sketches of the children.

A few weeks after Jeanne's horrid realisation of the passing time, the weaver handed her the scrolls. He politely turned his head away as tears of joy rolled down her cheeks. Marie, who was 'working late,' touched her shoulder. What joy to behold her children again, albeit on paper. How they had changed.

*

It was these drawings that she treasured most when the time came for her to make a move out of the kingdom.

She folded them carefully and slipped them into a leather wallet. Jacob's transfer from Cahors meant her presence in Villemade was no longer indispensable, and she realised it would create unnecessary risks for her host if she remained, especially in light of the punishment that awaited anyone found harbouring a Huguenot.

Not only that, but she sensed a nascent romance between

Monsieur Cordelle and Marie which the kind-hearted man felt visibly awkward about, given the difference in age. But Marie seemed available and willing, and he had been an heirless widower for long enough. Jeanne was gladdened by the thought that at least her stay had brought hopes of marriage to the girl who had given her so much of her time.

On a star-studded night in August, after a tearful farewell to Marie, who was working late, Jeanne left the Quercy plain for the first time in her life.

(iii)

The harbour was hardly a sight for sunken spirits, even though it lay still as a millpond.

As Jacob climbed down to the water's surface, where a rowboat was waiting, he saw it was in fact the most nauseating broth, thick with human sludge, floating matter of all sorts, and drowned rats.

The little Phocean town sprawled out westward of the port and up the hillside called Colline des Accoules. It was made up of a quaint confusion of three- and four-storey dwellings, where cords ran between upper-floor windows to accommodate row upon row of washing above the streets. The windmills, posted like white sentinels along the high ground, confirmed the wind was well up, which thankfully swept away the insalubrious pong.

But as Jacob took his place in the boat that faced east, his eyes were met with a coordinated display of grandeur in the form of the recently built galley arsenal, lit up by the westering sun. The immaculate buildings, some still under construction, stood as a stark contrast to the chaotic urbanisation of the town, and as a testimony to the king's magnificence.

The arsenal, purposely built for the construction of the king's galley fleet, was a pool of activity with carpenters, rope makers, joiners, sail makers, riggers, caulkers, riveters— a host of tradesmen and labourers required to build a galley ship. Once ferried to shore, Jacob was marched with the cortege of prisoners towards the white arsenal building.

Along the way, he saw with his own eyes a galley ship with its rows of great oars. He counted twenty-six on one side, which made fifty-two in all. The port harboured over twenty such vessels, whose slaves, if near enough, glanced at the newcomers, some with envy. For they knew that these Protestants were going to the New World, where they would at least be allowed to roam about unshackled; a galley slave could not.

There were Turks and common convicts whose complicit laughter expressed camaraderie. And then there were the downcast ones who looked on with a silent longing. There was always someone worse off than oneself, thought Jacob and, while continuing his march onward, closed his eyes just for two seconds. The moment he opened them again, they were seized by a familiar face on the greatest galley ship of all, la *Grande Réale*. The huge ship was manoeuvring only twenty yards from where Jacob was passing. The face stared back at him, and he recognised Monsieur Galet.

He was about to call out when the convert he met in his prison in Montauban gave a stern shake of the head. Delpech then realised there was no point in attracting unnecessary attention which would be beneficial to neither of them. Even from this distance, Jacob could read in the man's demeanour expressions of pity, shame, and remorse. He must have got caught trying to cross the frontier, he thought.

As Delpech marched past the galley ship, both men gave a hardly perceptible sign that bade each other God's grace and good fortune. They both knew they would probably never meet in this life again.

The cortege passed through the arsenal gates, over the impeccable courts strewn with cordage and sails, and past the workshops and depots stocked to the rafters with masts and timber.

They continued until they reached a large building which housed the galley slave hospital. They were then ushered into a large room already abuzz with two hundred men and women. They all constituted the next shipment for Saint Domingue, a French territory in the Caribbean Sea.

*

Jacob was exhausted from the voyage but glad to be able to rest on firm ground.

He wanted to mingle amid the strangers of every age, rank and condition, in the hope of hearing the unmistakable accent of his home town. But he had hardly the strength to stand up straight, and besides, he soon found himself in conversation with some fellow detainees from the tartan. He would go for a saunter tomorrow.

The guards were already lighting the night lamps, and sheeting was being drawn down across the middle of the ward to divide it into separate male and female sleeping quarters. The newcomers were given shabby straw mattresses, previously used by sick galley slaves, and ordered to find a place to settle or risk a hiding.

'Well, then, I shall bid you goodnight, Madame,' said Jacob to a lady of some distinction, with whom he had been sharing his first impressions. The vast room had just a few high windows and was scarcely less dismal than the round tower of Aigues-Mortes. But at least he had good company.

'May the Lord bring you rest, Sir,' said the lady.

Her name was Madame de Fontenay, seventy years old and fit as a fiddle. She was chaperoning Mademoiselle Marianne Duvivier, the demoiselle who had courageously held the sailor's gaze on board the tartan. Madame de Fontenay had literally fallen into conversation with Jacob during the voyage after he caught her as she stumbled. He had since taken it upon himself to watch over her and her granddaughter, although in truth, she had been more comfort to him during his seasickness than he to her.

Jacob said, 'I pray you find some sleep too, Madame.'

'Oh,' replied Madame de Fontenay with merriment in her voice, 'I have learnt to sleep with one eye open, for I shall have plenty of time to catch up on lost nights where I am headed.' She gave a fleeting glance upward as if she were peeping into heaven.

Jacob smiled, then bade goodnight to Mademoiselle Duvivier.

He set out his straw mattress against the wall and knelt in preparation for his evening prayer.

'Be careful when you pray here, my friend,' said a gentleman in a low voice next to him. The man, in his late fifties, could see that his new neighbour was one of the newcomers.

For his part, Jacob wondered if the man was a Huguenot

or a common prisoner, for he did not look as though he was going to say his prayers. But then, on looking around, Delpech realised that no one else was either. The man flicked his eyes up at the approaching guard, doing his rounds and carrying a hard wooden club.

'I see,' said Jacob, 'I shall wait till they extinguish the lights.'

'They don't,' said the man. 'And they don't let up doing their rounds neither . . .'

As they spoke, an old man with his back to them, ten yards in front, rose up on his knees in prayer. The guard bounded forward and cracked the man's joined knuckles with his long club. Jacob could not abide such a display of needless cruelty. Forgetting his fatigue, he stood up and shouted, 'How dare you, Sir!'

The guard turned. He strode swiftly with a limp towards Delpech and, holding his long truncheon with two hands, he thrust it under Jacob's chin, driving him against the whitewashed wall. Jacob was forced up onto his toes, which virtually left the ground, a testimony to how much weight he had lost.

In a low growl, the guard said: 'Don't you dare try to impede a king's guard from doing his duty. Try it again, and I'll have you seated in one of our galleys, quicker than you can say Pope Innocent XI! You got that?'

The old man who had been rapped on the knuckles was now standing a short distance behind the guard, gesturing to Jacob to let it drop, that it was not worth risking being sent to the galleys. But it was the guard's informal use of you that made Delpech see there was no point in arguing over an injustice with a man who lacked social etiquette.

Jacob had just met Arnaud Canet, chief guard, mid-thirties, a quick eye, powerful neck, and thick forearms.

*

Arnaud Canet had been a sailor on the high seas before losing a leg, crushed by a cannon when he was twenty-seven. He had since worked up through the ranks at the arsenal where he had guarded some of France's most treacherous villains, at least, the ones who had escaped the executioner's talents.

He had guarded a broad range of delinquents from petty thieves to infidels, and clandestine salt sellers to Algerian pirates. Criminals of every race, class, and colour had been paraded before Canet's unblinking eye, especially nowadays, what with the king's policy to enlarge his galley fleet. Indeed, the galley slave ships had grown in numbers from ten to thirty since he had started at the arsenal. The new trend was recruiting Protestants, though this batch was lucky: they were going to the American islands. But whatever his crime, a criminal was a criminal, and by far, the best and safest way to deal with criminals was to treat them all as scoundrels.

Canet knew from experience at sea that the only way to prevent mutiny was to nip it in the bud. So his guards, through fear of revolt or cocky courage, did their rounds in search of opportunities to brandish their clubs on man or woman, young or old, in order to stamp out potential firebrands and demagogues. If allowed to flourish, such hotheads could incite a movement of riot.

One such opportunity arose when the reformist convicts prayed on their knees to their Protestant god. Such an act had been banned and their god banished from the realm by the king himself. But for Jacob, like for every other Huguenot, prayer was the spiritual staple that kept him going. Being without it was like living without God, and that was every bit as insufferable as the dreadful conditions in scenes from Dante's *Inferno*.

So it presented the perfect occasion for the guards to lay down their authority.

However, these Protestants were not martyrs, and the group reflex was to discreetly gather round the kneeling co-religionists so forming a human screen. When one group went down, those standing around them tacitly moved close together to create a random ring three or four people deep.

By the second day, Jacob and the other newcomers had cottoned on. In this way, only rarely did the guards get a clean swipe at the recidivist worshippers.

But Canet was an old hand: it did not take long for him to suss out their tactics. He was nobody's fool.

'They're pissing in my boots, they are!' he said to his crew one day. Did these bourgeois really think they could pull the wool over the eyes of a battle-seasoned veteran and son of a tinker? So he told his guards to lie low for a few days, lead the lambs into a false sense of security.

'Then the wolves will pounce!' he said, punctuating his rallying talk in the guardroom with a gruff, vengeful growl.

*

Because of his altercation just after his arrival, Jacob had kept a sharper-than-usual eye on the guards, whose demeanour seemed to have changed slightly. He noticed they appeared to swagger more, and even turn a blind eye when people congregated.

'It may well be they were just setting down their law,' said Monsieur Blanchard, the gentleman who had warned Jacob about praying in the open.

'Yes,' said Jacob, scratching his six-day beard, 'I suppose their argument could be that it is always easier to begin with a tight rein, then loosen it, rather than the contrary.'

'They have tested us,' said Madame de Fontenay. 'Now they realise we are not to be treated as criminals.'

'Perhaps. Or perhaps not,' said Jacob musingly as he turned to eye an approaching guard, slapping his club in one hand in double time to his step.

*

The following morning, Canet told his guards the time had come to reap the rewards of the successful application of his plan.

'Prohibited action means punitive re-action!' he said, smashing his big, square fist into the wooden staff table.

He was looking forward to it: he had not cracked his stick over anyone's shoulder blades for two full days, and it was making him bearish, even to his wife. But she ought to know by now not to go on at a man when he was uptight. She would just have to avoid going out uncovered for a few days. He nonetheless regretted his slip of the hand, and even had to stifle a desire to blame the state for sending so many soft bourgeois pigeons through Marseille. As if he hadn't enough work with the usual crowd of galley slaves to break in. They, at least, put up a decent fight and had the mettle to take a fair battering for it.

So this morning, he was really looking forward to letting out the cats among the pigeons.

Their chosen tactic was to bide their time for a large

round of people to form. 'The more the merrier,' said one of the guards called Durand, a slim man of medium stature with a goatee beard.

After the Huguenots' meagre slops, and black bread from the arsenal bakery, Canet went on the prowl. He had to be extra careful to keep a little malicious smile from pleating the corners of his mouth. He must give nothing away; the surprise must be total.

Now that he had taken time to observe their little circus, he was easily able to identify a screen forming, despite their attempt at discretion. He did not have to wait for long before a large group was beginning to cluster near the middle of the ward. It was perfectly placed, allowing him and his guards to slowly surround it, and probably offered a good-size group of Huguenots to bash. He chuckled to himself at their naive attempt to conceal their manoeuvres. Some of them had even forgotten their prudence now that they had been given some leash, probably imagining that he and his guards were deliberately turning a blind eye to their law-breaking.

He gave the sign to Durand, who was ten paces away. It consisted of three slaps of the club in his hand, repeated twice. Durand signalled likewise to the next guard, and suddenly, Canet could feel a new tension in the air.

Within thirty seconds, he knew his guards would be in place. On the other side, the two guards began to centre on the group, and instinctively, Huguenots from Canet's side began to shuffle round to where the agitation was coming from. It was the cue. Now that the human wall on his side had thinned, he could bowl in. With authority and the stern use of his club, he quickly blazed a trail through the protesting crowd to the epicentre.

There, his eyes were met not with ten or fifteen suppliant Huguenots in the act of their crime, but with old Madame de Fontenay squatting over a bucket.

After the initial shock, Arnaud Canet roared his frustration through gritted teeth. 'So this is how you honour your god, is it, old woman?' he said as the other two guards pushed through to join him. They instinctively shielded their eyes in disgust. Canet continued. 'It does not surprise me your god accepts offerings of crap!'

'As you well observe, Monsieur, this is not a call of God; it is a call of nature,' corrected the old woman. 'Now, if you will excuse me. It is demeaning enough for a lady to the manor born to find herself squatting on the throne amid her brethren, let alone in the company of her jailers!'

The sham was the talk of the ward for the rest of the week, and guards became less inclined to break through the crowd, unnerved as they were by what they might find. Would those at the centre be kneeling or squatting? There were limits to even the coarsest sensibilities.

*

'I am not familiar with these ports of Midi,' said Jacob. 'I usually ship via Bordeaux or the northern ports. They present less of a risk of capture.'

'Indeed, Sir,' said Monsieur Blanchard, 'and I only hope we shall sail under good escort, for as you well know, the sea offshore is infested with Barbary pirates. I do not want to end up in the prisons of Mulay Ismail.'

'Goodness gracious, neither do I,' said Mademoiselle Duvivier, who shuddered at the thought of losing her virginity to a dark infidel.

They were talking about their imminent departure for America. They had been informed they would set sail on 18 September, in less than a week. It was held in higher spheres that letting them know in advance would make them more susceptible to conversion as the fateful date approached. But the high hopes of conversion only fed Canet's frustration: so far, the Huguenots had remained infuriatingly steadfast.

A little before lunchtime, Jacob was standing near the wall at the imaginary dividing line where both sexes mingled by day. He was in the company of his usual circle of new acquaintances which included Madame de Fontenay, Mademoiselle Duvivier, Monsieur Blanchard, and a few others. It was certainly a comfort to be among like-minded people as opposed to the solitude of his imprisonment in the dungeon of Cahors. To pass the time, they had each told their story, how their brutal fall from their station was like the earth trembling beneath their feet. Monsieur Blanchard had been a master periwig maker to the king before having to turn his hand to buying and selling, as did many a Huguenot deprived by law of their livelihood. Madame de Fontenay's deceased husband, landowner and aristocrat, had served the king in arms. She had been caught praying at a clandestine assembly with her granddaughter, Marianne Duvivier. Mademoiselle Duvivier's mother died in childbirth; her father fell at the Battle of Entzheim a few years later. Her grandmother was her only family.

The beating of a drum interrupted their conversation and silenced the chatter of the ward.

'Jacob Delpech de Castanet of Montauban, you are asked to manifest yourself,' called out Canet's voice above the crowd.

A rush of anxiety sped through Jacob's veins, causing him to become almost out of breath. Could Robert have managed a last- minute reprieve?

'Over here, Sir,' Jacob called out.

Arnaud Canet limped through the parting crowd with a bounce in his step and a malicious rictus.

'Sir,' he said, 'are you the father of one Louise Delpech?'

The name of Jacob's daughter seemed to take him back an eternity. He had not seen her for two full years, since Jeanne escaped through the gate of Montauban with Lulu on her lap. Robert had recounted to him in a letter the whole episode of Jeanne's determination to protect her children. Now, life before the dragonnade seemed like a dream. He had never forgotten that poor Jeanne and his children had also been living a nightmare, and he had prayed every day for their safety and well-being. *Of course they are well. Of course they are all right*, he would constantly repeat in his mind between conversations, before his prayers, and before sleep, to chase away morbid thoughts of their suffering, suffering which he could not witness or temper.

'I am, Sir,' said Jacob with a sudden sickness in his heart. Canet loved to see a bourgeois deflate with fear.

'I am to inform you she's dead.'

Jacob turned white. 'Sir, please,' he said before the guard turned on his heels, 'are you certain?'

'Can you read the king's French?'

Jacob could only find the strength to nod.

'Cop that, then; keep it as a souvenir from Marseille.'

Canet turned with total satisfaction, and continued on his round.

Jacob's eyes fell on the note. Then he collapsed.

131

(iv)

By 1687, the passion for Protestant persecution had abated a little, which made Jeanne's escape more feasible, though it was not without risk. It was a time of exodus for thousands of converts who could no longer bear to live as impostors, and who often gave up their worldly possessions for the sake of a free conscience.

Since the Revocation, a network had sprung up along the roads of exile. A multitude of guides offered their services to fleeing Huguenots. And although the authorities were as keen as ever to prevent tradesmen and academics from leaving the country, they simply did not have the policing resources to do so.

Nonetheless, if Jeanne was to stand a chance of escaping to Geneva, she had to have a good guide, Robert had concluded, even if it cost the astronomic sum of two thousand livres. It was a small fortune, the price of the farmhouse where Jeanne first found refuge. But it could later be taken out of the children's inheritance, which the state would legally have to one day honour. And anyway, if the money could not be recovered, Robert considered it a small price to pay for appeasing his own conscience.

Jeanne followed the weaver on mule-back. It was a long and scary night journey to Villefranche in Rouergue. But the warm night air and her newfound freedom after sixteen months in hiding helped her overcome her fears of capture. They rode over flat country to Caussade, before passing into the limestone hills of Quercy. Then on they travelled by Caylus, and along the gorges of the province of Rouergue.

They arrived at Villefranche on schedule, an hour after

daybreak. Outside the bastide city, they stopped at an inn run by a former Huguenot, where a guide, a thickset man of average height and few words, was waiting at a table near the window with two other evacuees who sat in silence. His wide-brimmed hat still obscured his weather-worn face. And beneath an aquiline nose, Jeanne noted his bushy moustache was beginning to turn grey. The name he gave was David Trouvier.

Jeanne had learnt enough patois to pass for a peasant; nevertheless, something compelled her to speak to her new guide in French, as if to assert her true status. Despite having occupied many a night learning how to spin thread and weave cloth to make herself useful to Monsieur Cordelle, she had not lost her ingrained sense of social rank.

It at first surprised her to discover how insignificant she had become, dressed as she was in Marie's clothing: a blue skirt, white blouse, laced bonnet, and a shawl for night travel. Nobody among the departing voyagers and travelling merchants had given a second turn of the head when she had walked into the inn.

Yet she had grown as a woman, become more worldly in her lower-class garb, even though her gait was still one of a manor-born lady, poised and erect, and without the stoop of the peasant. She had conditioned herself not to give in to melancholy or doubt, but to be strong and determined to bring her family back together. This was what fuelled her resolution to get to Geneva, where there would be hope.

She had developed such a deep understanding of the peasant's way of life that when the other two evacuees first set eyes on her, they must have wondered how in the world a country woman could pay the price of the passage to

Geneva. Only when she lowered her shawl to reveal her head carriage and they heard her talk did they realise her true condition. Jeanne gave a discreet smile and nodded at the two young people. He was a cabinetmaker by the name of Etienne Lambrois, and was accompanied by his sister, whom he introduced as Mademoiselle Claire. It gave both ladies reassurance to find another woman among their little party, and they sat down together on the bench.

However, few words were exchanged between them. It was the advice given by Trouvier, so that if anyone got caught, they would reveal little or nothing of their fellow travellers.

Monsieur Cordelle took refreshment with the party. Then he headed back to Villemade, saddened but relieved that he had done his duty by Monsieur Garrisson, and with a rush of blood to be going back to Marie.

*

Jeanne and her new companions travelled by night, taking refuge come morning in a landscape of deep valleys and steep gorges.

On three occasions, they were able to halt at a remote inn or a safe house owned by resolute Huguenots determined to remain in the rocky range. But mostly, they sheltered by day in barns, granaries, shepherd's huts, and in the woods off the beaten track of patrolling soldiers. There, they would pray, take refreshment, and rest their aching bones. It was the right season to travel, and if all went well, they would be in Geneva well ahead of the first snowfall.

The talents of the cabinetmaker were put to good use, building a temporary shelter on the rare times it rained. It quickly became clear to Jeanne by their furtive gestures that Etienne and Claire were not siblings: they were lovers, she was sure. What drama had they left behind them? No doubt they wondered the same about her, but all persons present had vowed only to speak of the task at hand, which sometimes made Jeanne almost feel as young as Claire again.

One mid-September morning, Jeanne let out a gasp of surprise as they emerged from a dim mountain pass and halted at a gap in the vegetation. The sun was rising brightly over an expanse of softly rolling hills abounding with terraced vineyards and fields of lavender. Claire, though exhausted, gave a wheeze of delight. They had reached the Rhone valley.

'Halfway there,' said the guide, breaking the silence in his slow country accent. The ladies admired the clear view while Trouvier raised his arm and pointed to the left of the sun. 'From here, we follow the river to Seyssel,' he said.

Etienne Lambrois, who had been keeping up the rear, halted his mule and said, 'I was given to understand that we could pass into Orange country by crossing the bridge at Saint-Esprit. That is to the right of the sun, is it not?'

'If you have a passport, you can cross,' said Trouvier.

'Can't we slip a guard a louis d'or?'

'Some you can, some you can't, some you never know. I prefer not to take the risk.'

'Seyssel is only a few days from Geneva, is it not?' asked Jeanne, who had heard the name before, no doubt during dinner conversations with her husband's customers.

'Yes, it be that, Madame,' said Trouvier.

'But that would mean another three weeks on French soil,' said Etienne.

135

There was indulgence in Trouvier's voice when he turned in his saddle and said, 'Which is better than a lifetime on a galley ship, is it not?'

'As long as we do not get caught now that the terrain is more open,' said Jeanne, to soften the guide's natural ascendancy over the young man.

But the young cabinetmaker was still visibly wrestling with a dilemma. After a moment, he said, 'Don't get me wrong, but how can we be sure we are not being led astray, into the hands of the king's men? There is a good reward for delivering Protestants.'

'If I were that way inclined,' said the guide, 'I'd have taken you over the bridge at Saint-Esprit. It's where they catch many an unwary traveller. Now, we'd better get to a safe house before we're seen by all the world and his wife.'

The guide dug in his heels and rode on down the track. Jeanne and the clandestine couple followed behind.

11

Mid to Late September 1687

LATE AFTERNOON ON 18 September, Jacob squinted as he stepped into the daylight.

He was being led out of the obscure hospital ward with nineteen other Protestant prisoners. His body felt stiff and his face still twinged from his fall onto the stone floor the week before. But the deep blue sky was like a therapy for the eyes. And he was relieved that his group included his small cast of friends.

Port activity was resuming, following the afternoon siesta imposed by the sultry heat. The group shuffled through the arsenal yards to the harbour, where two galley ships were still in construction. Jacob remarked how they had progressed since he first saw them. One was already being fitted with its ornate figurehead, which meant it was almost ready for its crew of two hundred and fifty slaves whose living, eating, and toilet quarters would be the bench they were assigned to.

Around the animated port, seasoned slaves were already knitting or sewing in the long galley ships. A few trustee convicts were busy at small stalls posted mostly on the west side of the harbour, where their galleys were moored. Apart from the shaved heads topped with red bonnets, these men were recognisable by the limp caused by the ball chained to their ankle, or by the chain that attached them to their stand. They were, however, the lucky ones, allowed to serve out their time by offering their wares and know-how to port visitors by day, and returning to their galley bench come evening-tide.

They exercised a multitude of trades from cobbler to wig maker, and made anything from straw boxes to small pieces of furniture, pipes, wood sculptures, and figurines made of shells. Some offered an astonishing assortment of services from letter writing to producing certificates stamped with fake seals, all under the knowing eye of the king's police.

But there were no Protestants among these privileged few; even in servitude, Huguenots were deprived of any sort of relief. Not only had their personal fortunes been added to the king's treasury, they were given worse treatment than the basest of criminals.

The group continued past horses pulling winches, dockers unloading Caribbean cargo, and officers barking commands. Well-heeled ladies and gentlemen who must have recently disembarked were directing their effects onto carts that waited among wine baskets and barrels of sugarloaf, cocoa, tobacco, and ginger. The port water was thronged with boats, galleys, tall ships, and seagulls pecking into sludge. But the windmills on the crest of land above the harbour stood motionless, and the place stank of fish, salt, seaweed, horses, and humanity.

It was nonetheless a stirring sight, though one which induced an anxious silence among the prisoners as they neared their embarkation point. In the calm water that shimmered like a silken lake, Jacob saw a pink—a square-rigged merchantman—and a larger ship, both anchored a short distance from the foreshore. He could make out that the smaller vessel was called La Marie, the larger one *La Concorde*.

'One of those, I believe, is to be our home for the coming months,' he said, turning to Mademoiselle Duvivier. She instinctively placed her hand on her chest as the notion sunk in that they really were about to embark on a voyage to the other side of the world.

They had walked out of the dim hospital ward together. Mademoiselle Duvivier and Madame de Fontenay had been angels to Jacob since the terrible shock which caused him to collapse. The young girl had nursed his brow, cut in the fall on the flagstone floor, and they had comforted him with prayer to mend his broken spirit.

They were standing in the middle of the line; behind them were Madame de Fontenay and Monsieur Blanchard.

'I wonder which,' said the girl.

'The bigger the ship, the better she sits in the sea, I have heard it said,' said Monsieur Blanchard.

'Well, the closest is *La Marie*,' said Madame de Fontenay. 'I am sorry to say—'

'Oy!' roared Canet. 'No talking in the ranks!' he bayed, limping back down the file. 'Unless you wanna feel my stick!'

A minute later found them at the embarkation point, where the head of the line began boarding a longboat. It was soon Jacob's turn to place a foot on the gangplank, slippery with sludge. With her bundle of effects strapped to her back, the girl lifted her skirts above her shoes, took his hand over the gangplank, then lowered herself into the boat. He then held out his hand for Madame de Fontenay.

By now Canet, standing three yards away, was losing patience; such gentility made him want to puke. And besides, he still hadn't had the last laugh on the old duchess. So he lunged forward and held out his stick like a turnstile in front of her.

'Halt there,' he commanded. Then with a snarl of triumph, to Jacob he said: 'You. Get in!'

While detaining Madame de Fontenay and Monsieur Blanchard, he told the prisoners behind to proceed into the longboat.

It took a moment for Jacob and Marianne to realise what was happening. Then the girl called out in a tone of voice that conveyed her sudden anxiety. 'Grandmother!'

Against the flow of the incoming prisoners, she hoisted herself back onto the gangplank. Madame de Fontenay still looked confused and reached out her hand to her granddaughter.

'Put her in the boat!' called Canet to a subordinate guard, while pushing back the old lady with his stick, held in two hands.

'Get back in the boat!' hurled the guard, whose deep bark would make any man shake in boots. But Marianne Duvivier persisted. Jacob reached her before the guard could use his stick. He placed himself in front of the girl.

'Sir,' he said to Canet, trying to keep his voice reasonable and calm. 'The lady is the child's grandmother.'

'That, you Protestant ponce, is why we are separating them,' roared Canet, spraying his bitterness into Jacob's face.

'Now do as you're soddin' told!'

Before Jacob could answer back, a sharp pain on his right upper arm made him cow down. He turned in time to see the second guard, raising his stick to carry out a correction commonly known as a *bastonnade*, which was a series of blows normally inflicted on obstinate galley slaves. But Jacob retreated down the plank, forcing the girl back behind him.

'Grandmother!' she cried in a fit of hysteria. However, Madame de Fontenay, being of a practical nature, understood that the scene could quickly degenerate. She pushed out her palms as if to push the girl away, and cast an imploring look at Jacob which needed no words.

She knew she might not survive the voyage herself anyway— then what would become of the girl? Monsieur Delpech was a good man; he would take care of her, give her protection day and night in the den of vigorous sailors. Was this not then God's intention? In return, she was sure that taking care of the girl would take his mind off the dark thoughts he had been having since the death of his child.

'Stay with Monsieur Delpech,' she called to Marianne.

Jacob gave the old lady a nod to confirm he would take good care of her granddaughter, though he secretly wondered how. He took hold of the girl's arms before she could battle with the guard to get past. With a firm grip, he turned her back towards the boat.

'Come, Marianne, there is no use fighting them; you will only make things worse,' he said. 'We will see your grandmother again when we arrive, on the other side.' Jacob realised the ambiguity of his words, but did not try to correct them.

It was a cruel and needless separation, designed to cripple

more than any blow of the stick. The intention was to wrench a conversion from either grandparent or grandchild, even though it was widely accepted that once a Huguenot had come this far, there was very little chance of them abjuring.

Mademoiselle Duvivier suddenly seemed so frail, and she let him guide her. She looked back over her shoulder as her grandmother stood dignified on the foreshore. Madame de Fontenay stared back with passion in her eyes in a last effort to impress her obstinate resolution onto her granddaughter.

They continued into the longboat. 'Keep by me, my girl,' said Jacob. It was best to make the longboat crew assume they were related in some way. A lass on her own was always easy prey, and some shipmen would not think twice about trying it on. Catching on, she gave him a nod and pressed herself closer to him. But this did not impress the handsome sailor leaning against his punt, and he instinctively ogled the young female as she passed.

The longboat was soon breaking the silky film on the water's surface as it ferried the forlorn passengers to the place they would inhabit for the next five months.

*

La Marie was a three-mast vessel of two hundred tons.

Jacob did not know much about ships, but he did know that this type of vessel with its shallow draught was more commonly used for transporting cargo around the Mediterranean coast than for crossing the great ocean sea. She was smaller than La Concorde, the tall ship that Madame de Fontenay and Monsieur Blanchard were to board.

The space below deck was partitioned into five rooms. At the stern was the captain's and officers' cabin. Next came the sailors' and the soldiers' quarters. The third room was where common prisoners were kept chained. This was followed by a room that housed seventy galley slaves, men of every colour, Turks as well as Christians, also cuffed in heavy chains. Too old or too ill for service, these broken men were sent to America to be sold.

The last compartment was situated under the kitchen at the front of the vessel. This was reserved for the Huguenots. It was so small that twenty people would have been pushed for space, yet there were close to eighty Protestant prisoners. Two-thirds men, one-third women, all were driven into the hole barely high enough to stand up in. Neither was there room to stretch out the length of one's body without lying on someone else.

Calling to mind how the hospital ward was divided at night, Jacob took the precaution to settle in the middle along one side so that he and the girl could remain within whispering distance. He noticed that the portholes were their only direct outlet to daylight, and realised the crossing would be more insufferable than any hole he had been made to suffer so far. He nevertheless thanked God for his previous preparation. He knew he would have stood little chance of surviving this scabrous den without it.

As he settled into his thoughts, with his back against the timber, there came screams and reports of rats crawling among the buckets placed at either end of the room. *How many months can we endure in this squalor and sickness?* he wondered.

But he vowed for the love of Jeanne and his children he

would not give up, for the love of Christ he would not doubt. And he would not let Mademoiselle Duvivier abandon herself to defeat either. As she sat beside him, looking distant and downcast, he took her small hand, placed it like a small bird in his large palm, and gave it a pat of encouragement.

'There is one consolation,' he said. 'Things can only get better from now on.'

She put on a brave smile, but she knew as well as he did that in truth, their crossing the wilderness had only just begun.

*

Thudding, scuffing, and rolling sounds were heard well into the night as the last of the provisions were hoisted aboard and stored.

With her belly full and her load carefully balanced, La Marie set sail the following day with *La Concorde* for Toulon, which was a day's voyage eastward along the coast. This was the rendezvous of their escort, two warships, without which they would be easy pickings for Barbary pirates.

The heat generated by eighty people crammed like sardines in a barrel did nothing to help Jacob find his sea legs. He spent most of the time trying to slumber, in the hope of waking to find his body had become accustomed to the constant roll of the ship. But sleep, too, eluded him.

Nevertheless, the run into Toulon, gruelling though it was, passed without incident. Come nightfall, the calm port waters that gently rocked the pink made a welcome change from the commotion of the previous nights. And the

Huguenot hole soon resounded with the sounds of sleepers snorting and snoring, some coughing, tossing, and turning, among the audacious rats rummaging for anything to sink their teeth into.

Late into the night, the clouds dissipated, letting white moonlight shine in through the portholes. And the cooler air that whisked round the room took the edge off the stifling heat, not to mention the stench.

One old man was still trying to sleep with his palm on his ear to block out the intolerable noise of sleepers, when he felt something nip his finger. He gave a yelp, and swiped the rat on the end of it. The obnoxious creature landed on Jacob Delpech's thigh, glared its annoyance at its aggressor, and then scampered off in search of another opportunity.

Whisperings at the door, a dimly lit oil lantern, and the turn of a key announced the late-night round of a guard. He found the Protestants sleeping top and tail, mostly. There was hardly any space for him to put his feet without treading on parts of their anatomy, which he was very careful to avoid. He stepped from one space to another like on stepping stones in a quagmire of bodies. At last he reached the object of his midnight jaunt.

He stared down at the young girl who had caught his eye in the longboat two days earlier. He had since been eyeing her movements, her mannerisms, smiling at her when it was his turn to take away the buckets, and had decided she was too sweet to suffer being squashed against these smelly bodies every night.

The old geezer did not fool him either; anyone could tell they were not that close, probably not even related. This sailor was not born with the last tide: this sailor had seen such a charade before. Why was it that some pompous codgers thought young girls wanted locking away when what they truly craved was to be properly loved? So he would do her the honour of taking her on deck for some clean air. The night was perfect, quite warm and starry now, and the captain was on shore.

He bent down and touched her arm gently, almost so as not to wake her. How beautiful she was, how nice it felt to touch a tight-skinned young woman. He had been longing for this, and now imagined cupping her firm breasts in his hands like plump little birds. At that instant, he felt love. He had to be careful though; he had to gain her trust first, then he would be able to tame her, make her his little lady for the duration of the cruise.

He now clasped the ball of her shoulder and shook her a little more firmly, brushing her warm jaw with his index finger with every nudge forward.

'Mademoiselle,' he whispered. 'Mademoiselle.'

She moved her head slightly, which brought a crafty smile to the corner of his mouth. Clearly, she was making the most of it. Then she opened her eyes wide. She turned, let out a short gasp.

'Shhh, Mademoiselle,' he whispered before any sound came out of her. 'Don't alarm yourself; I've come to take you to somewhere nicer.'

She looked wide-eyed, astonished, and speechless at the handsome face lit up by the yellow glow of the lamp. She did not want to disturb her co-religionists, exhausted as they were from the short voyage. The first days were always the worst until one found one's sea legs, she remembered her grandmother saying.

'I beg your pardon, Sir,' she said.

The fact that she kept to an intimate whisper gave the young man all the more confidence to proceed with his plan.

'Come, Mademoiselle,' he said with gentle authority and a handsome smile that showed his white teeth. 'I will show you the deck. The sky is beautiful tonight. Come.' He held out his hand to her. 'You will be perfectly safe with me.'

The young man was no stranger to her anymore. She had remarked on previous occasions that he was well-mannered, nice to look at, and inspired confidence, quite the opposite of the vulgar sailor on that tartan. Not quite knowing what else to do, she took his hand, and got to her feet.

'Be careful where you tread,' he said considerately, and led her gently over the piles of bodies. She was already receptive; it would not take him long to take her under his wing, though he had to admit, he never expected her to come round so quickly.

Jacob was snoring loudly on the gentlemen's side of the room. But then a twinge of pain from the arm that had received the blow from Canet's guard interrupted his sleep. He woke vaguely, turned around, and saw it was only the old man poking him. No doubt to stop Jacob's snoring; Jeanne used to do it all the time. But the old man nudged him again with insistence. Turning over, Jacob saw he was stabbing the darkness with his index finger.

'What is it, Sir?' he said in a whisper and glanced in the direction the man was pointing. It took a moment for Jacob to realise that the dark shapes moving a few yards in front of him were that of the girl following a guard. He quickly got to his feet. Striding with difficulty towards them, he said:

'Where are you going?'

'None of your business, pal,' said the sailor nonchalantly. 'You get back to sleep now.'

'Sir, I ask you to leave the girl; she is under my responsibility.'

'No, she ain't, you only just met her.' He took hold of the girl's hand. 'Take no notice of him,' he said to her gently.

But the girl stopped; the sailor tugged her forward.

'No you don't, young man,' said Jacob, raising his voice. 'Any further and I shall call for the captain!'

By now people were beginning to stir; two or three of them were sitting up on their elbows, trying to fathom out what was going on. More people began to groan as Jacob stepped hurriedly towards the door to intercept the young guard. The girl was now struggling to get her hand free.

The magical moment, that window of serenity, was quickly closing for the sailor, all because of an interfering Huguenot. What an old codger, standing in the way of youth! The sailor let go of the girl, and put down his lantern.

He then lunged forward, seizing Jacob by the shirt front with one hand, and clobbering him on the side of the face with the other. He was strong and vigorous, and furious now that the Huguenot had messed everything up. Jacob could not fight back without the risk of being sent to the room next door for the remainder of the voyage. Besides, his hands were more used to turning the smooth pages of a ledger than gripping rough rope as were the sailor's. Another blow sent him stumbling backwards, and he tripped on someone lying behind. Sleepers woke and scattered. The sailor followed through with a boot in the ribs as Jacob endeavoured to protect himself by crawling into a ball.

By now the whole room had twigged the scene that was

being played out in the darkness. There was a collective uproar of protest which was as loud as it was sudden, as if everyone in the room understood what was going on at the same time.

'Any more of your lip, pal, and I'll throw you next door!' hurled the sailor, who had taken up his lantern. He edged backwards the few yards to the barred timber door where a fellow guard was waiting for him.

Before Jacob could reply, the sailor slipped out, and a key was clunking in the door lock.

Mademoiselle Duvivier rushed to help Jacob back to his feet.

'What got into you, girl?' he said, still panting from the assault.

'I am sorry. I—I don't know,' she stuttered, 'I—I did not know what to do.'

How senseless she had been, like she was caught in a trance, like some sovereign force was compelling her forward, disabling her to think for herself. But now she knew what to do if any man tried to lead her away again. She would resist and scream at the top of her voice, she told Jacob.

'Yes, do that, my girl,' said Jacob. By now several people were around him, arms helping him back to his place.

'We must get word to the captain,' said one man, an aging surgeon named Bourget.

'It is simply outrageous!' said Madame Fesquet, a middle-aged matron, who was comforting the girl.

'We will not be treated as animals,' said another man.

But what could they do? The captain was hardly sympathetic to their cause; on the contrary. He visibly allowed his men to hurl the most obscene language at them, as if it were a contest to string together the most melodious and injurious insult.

'We shall have to set up a night watch,' said Jacob. 'They will not try to carry out their detestable designs if we all stand together.'

*

Come morning, Joseph Reners, merchant and master of *La Marie* after God, was on his way back to the ship after spending the night in Toulon.

He had met with the captain of *La Concorde* and the commander of the two warships that were to escort them to Cadiz via Gibraltar. Then they would sail on to the Canaries to pick up the trade winds that would take them across the ocean to the Caribbean Sea. It had been agreed they would set sail the day after tomorrow. But a tragedy came about later that morning that would delay their plans.

The wind had picked up slightly, and blew fresh air into the Huguenot cabin, which was much appreciated. The buckets still had not been emptied, and the place stank of sick, excrement, and gruel.

'I say,' said Madame Fesquet, who was looking out of a porthole, 'that looks like the scoundrel from last night.' She beckoned Mademoiselle Duvivier over to see.

'Yes, that is him,' said Marianne, peering at the longboat as it approached on the lee side of the pink out of the blustery wind.

The culprit was rowing with another sailor behind Captain Reners. Marianne Duvivier could see that he had not changed at all: he looked just as robust and confident as before his outrageous behaviour of the previous night.

As the boat came closer, the young man looked up at the front of the pink, where the Huguenot cabin was situated, and he blew a kiss to the porthole. Shocked and shamefaced, the girl brought her head out of view and stood with her back pinned against the timber wall. Her heart was racing. She was suddenly petrified of the man's audacity.

The first officer changed places in the longboat with the captain. It had been agreed that the second in command would go ashore after the master.

Marianne said nothing of the kiss. Instead, she lingered near the porthole, grateful for the change of air. The next time she looked out, the longboat was already halfway to shore.

Jacob was trying to think how he could tell the captain about the incident of the night before, when a sudden gust kicked into the ship's starboard, causing the vessel to tilt to one side slightly. It did nothing to ease Jacob's aching head or his unstable belly; in fact, he nearly threw up.

Mademoiselle Duvivier, who was still peering out of the porthole, suddenly gasped. 'Oh, my God!' she shrieked in spite of herself.

At the same time, a sailor's voice from the deck above shouted: 'Man overboard!' This was surprising, given that they were anchored, and the sea, though not still, was not rough. Above deck, the sound of scurrying feet rumbled through the timber on the port side of the ship that looked onto the quay. Despite his aching body, Jacob managed to lift himself up and get a peek through the porthole at the longboat that had just keeled over. It had turned turtle under the force of a freak wave, and there was nothing anyone could do.

It became evident that the first mate and the two sailors could not swim. It was of the general opinion among seafarers that it was better to drown quickly than to suffer cold and a prolonged agony at the mercy of sharks and other creatures of the deep. However, in this case, it would have saved their lives had they known how to swim just a few yards to the floating oars. After a short struggle, under the eyes of both crew and prisoners, one after the other, the three men slipped under.

Was it maternal instinct, was it her faith, or was it something else? For some strange reason which she preferred not to understand, the girl felt deeply grieved for the handsome sailor who would surely have tried to abuse her innocence again had he lived. She prayed that he may rest in peace, if it so pleased God.

Stupid way to die, thought Jacob. How treacherous was the sea, even in mild weather. However, he felt no remorse for the young sailor who had tried to steal the girl away to satisfy his own illicit lust, and who had given him a hiding for interposing. For the first time, Jacob could not bring himself to pray for forgiveness for a man's sins. Nor could he pray that God Almighty would enable the young man's soul to receive His light if it so pleased Him. Instead, he gave thanks for their deliverance from malice.

The tragic accident meant that replacements had to be found, which delayed the departure.

After ten long days in Toulon harbour, *La Marie* and *La Concorde*, escorted by the king's warships, at last set sail on their voyage to America.

12

October 1687

JEANNE RODE UP with her travelling companions to the right-bank hillside that overlooked the village of Seyssel.

Being the last upstream village on the navigable stretch of the Rhone, it was both a landing dock and an embarkation point. Passengers travelling from Geneva could continue their journey by boat downstream as far as Marseille. Those travelling upstream could disembark on the left bank and carry on by land to Geneva.

The October sky had turned purple; local folk knew that as soon as the wind dropped, the low clouds would shed their load. Boat people on the far bank were frantically unloading parcels, crates, and barrels that were tightly packed on a boat towed by horse from Lyon.

Jeanne cast her gaze over the nearest bank of the village, with its medieval church spire, tall stone buildings, and warehouses along the quay where a cargo ferry was being loaded. Trouvier explained that the old wooden bridge that joined the village had not yet been rebuilt following its recent collapse into surging waters. The ferry was at present the only means to get to the other side. By consequence, although excise was still carried out on the other side, customs checks on travellers were not so stringent because anybody could walk around the checkpoint through the vegetation further downstream. All eyes then stared eagerly straight ahead.

'Savoyard country,' said Trouvier, nodding to the wooded hillside of fir trees and the distant mountain peaks. 'Once over the towpath on the other side, we'll be in the Duchy of Savoy. Then it's just a couple of days to Geneva.'

*

David Trouvier knew on first glimpse of the river that the visible urgency near the water was not only due to the imminent rainfall.

It was because the river had already risen by two yards, which was unusual for the time of year. He guessed there must have been torrential rainstorms further upstream, where fast-running water that fell from the mountainsides increased the river's volume and velocity.

He knew, too, that tree trunks and branches could cause natural barrages, and that when these barrages broke, they could release a surge of water capable of flooding a town in minutes.

The river at Seyssel had burst its banks in the past. Trouvier knew that when it did, it became too perilous to even consider a crossing. But worse than that, the *bac-à-traille*, the reaction ferry that carried goods from one side to the other, would inevitably be smashed to pieces by debris and tree trunks carried downstream by the coursing water.

The company sheltered with their mules in a barn, where they prayed. Then they drank watered-down wine and ate dry sausage, bread, and cheese, while waiting for night to fall. It was cold outside, the coldest it had been since Jeanne rode out from Villemade that warm August evening. She and her companions were thankful they had purchased warmer clothing and leathers for the change of season when they had passed through a small town outside Lyon.

At three o'clock, the clouds broke. Trouvier glanced out at the drizzle from the barn door. He looked north: a leaden ceiling blotted out the sky. To the east, the closest mountains were no longer visible behind the mist. He turned to the company, who were resting on a three-legged log stool, a broken barrel, and the shaft of a hay wagon. He said, 'If there's a flood, we might still be here when the first snows fall.'

Jeanne leaned over on her stool and glanced through the door that the guide held ajar. In all simplicity, she said, 'Why can we not cross now?'

'Guards patrol come rain or shine, Madame.'

'Surely they will be occupied elsewhere with the bad weather,' said Etienne, joining David at the door.

'Maybe. Maybe not,' the guide said, and turned his face dubiously back towards the sky. The penalty for guiding Huguenots through France was death by hanging. If caught, at least he would not have to suffer the misery of rowing with Turks and bandits for the rest of his life.

'But Monsieur Trouvier, we will certainly be denounced if we remain here too long,' said Jeanne, who suppressed a longing to plead with the man now that freedom was within eyeshot.

Half an hour later, Trouvier, who could not resist being spoken to as an equal by the fair lady, was down by the river.

It was barely a hundred yards wide at this point. He was in conversation with the ferryman, whose flat-bottomed vessel was already loaded with tools, crates, and barrels of wine.

The *bac-à-traille* was attached by its mast to a single line that ran from bank to bank. This allowed the boatman to navigate across the river by angling the boat so it presented a slanted flank to the current which propelled the vessel forward.

The drizzle was nothing more than a nuisance to the ferryman, a big fellow in middle age with a large, weather-browned face under the wide brim of a leather hat.

'Ah, but there be four of us,' said David.

'Too risky, water's high, river's fast, can't take more than two,' said the boatman, handling a crate with his large hands.

David sensed the man was a Protestant sympathiser; otherwise, he would not have offered to take any at all. Trouvier said nothing, instead wheeled a barrel from the shore up the gangplank to the edge of the boat.

The boatman, having placed the crate, turned to catch hold of the barrel. 'I've another crossing yet before the day's done.' He nodded to a stack of tiles and more barrels of Seyssel wine waiting further back on the shore. 'I can ferry the other two on the next run.' He began rolling the barrel, then growled back, ''Course, long as we don't get a surge!'

The guide went back to the group standing under an old plane tree with the mules. Jeanne suggested the young couple should embark first; it would be more sensible for the guide to be the last to leave. She would not hear of the cabinetmaker giving up his place to allow the two women to cross together; besides, their mules might need a man's strength to calm them in case of a swirl. And he could help the boatman unload and reload on the other side, the quicker the better.

The clandestine lovers boarded and crossed without mishap. The rain continued to fall softly, though thunder in the hills announced that the river might not be negotiable for very long.

As soon as the ferry came back, the boatman, a warehouse worker, and Trouvier unloaded the barrels that contained cheese, butter, and fruit from Savoy. Then they loaded the tiles, barrels of French wine, and wheat destined for Geneva.

Jeanne counted time, out of sight in the shelter of the barn. With no knowledge of loading boats, if she tried to help, she would only get in the way. And as Monsieur Trouvier pointed out, it would be suspect, to say the least, to see a woman loading barrels onto the *bac-à-traille*. She spent the time thinking of her children, of where Jacob could be now, and of her life before the Revocation. On the approach of footsteps, she quickly folded her drawings and placed them neatly into her leather wallet.

'We must make haste, Madame,' said Trouvier at the door. 'The ferry will soon be primed to leave.'

Daylight was beginning to fade by the time she and her guide led their mules onto the raft. As the ferryman pushed away from the shallows with his punt, Jeanne and Trouvier turned simultaneously at the sound of approaching hooves.

Soldiers. Two of them.

Jeanne's heart stopped. She was barely a hundred yards from freedom. How could she be caught after so much effort, having tried so hard?

Her anxious eyes met those of the guide, who said, 'Remember, you are my wife.' She gave a half nod. 'Let me do the talking,' he said, stroking his moustache to hide his speech. 'If they hear you, we're both done for.'

Jeanne quashed a desire to pay the ferryman to go faster, and a temptation to plead for mercy. Instead, she steeled her nerves and focused her thoughts on her role as peasant wife. She adopted a stooped stance, which wasn't difficult after six weeks on mule-back.

The soldiers approached the little wooden jetty and commanded the boater to stop punting. They rode into the water up to the flat-bottomed boat on the downstream side so that it protected them from the splash of the flow. Their stirrups were just twelve inches above the water's surface.

'What are you carrying?' said the younger of the horsemen.

'Usual, Sir,' said the ferryman, 'wheat, tiles, and barrels of wine.'

'Why are you taking passengers?'

'Been visiting family, Sir,' said David before the boater could answer. 'On our way home.'

'Your passport paper.'

Under the force of the current, the boat bobbed. David reached over the edge and passed his passport to the officer. It was a fake, but a good one, and the seal on the letter was genuine.

'Where you from?'

'Rumilly, Sir. Been visiting the wife's sister.'

'There is a bridge further downstream. Why are you crossing here?'

'To save time. It's only three leagues from Seyssel.'

'Huguenots have been found trying to cross, thinking we are too busy to patrol here,' said the soldier with a hint of sarcasm. Jeanne's heart pounded so hard, she could hear its pulse in her ears despite the rush of the river.

'Your wife's passport,' said the soldier, steadying his horse.

Jeanne looked in bewilderment to Trouvier.

'Your papers. This!' snapped the guard, waving Trouvier's forged permit to travel. 'Where is your passport paper?'

What could she do? For a moment, her mind was numbed.

Trouvier suspected he was about to be arrested, which meant he would hang by the first snowfall. He stood, smiling up at the young soldier, wondering if he had a devil's chance of reaching his arm. No, he was not ready to swing yet. For ninety yards to freedom, he was prepared to kill a man, or be killed. It could not be much different from slicing a lamb's throat. He slowly placed his hand on his sheathed skinning knife tucked under his belt, and waited for the right moment.

Jeanne, meanwhile, opened her travelling sack. 'Boudiou, boudiou,' she said in Occitan, which in French meant Good God. She was not taking His name in vain. She was praying for a miracle.

Her hand fell upon her leather wallet. She had an idea.

She reached over to pass the wallet to the soldier's outstretched hand. Trouvier clasped his knife handle, but then a timely gust kicked into the stacked cargo and made the boat dip. Jeanne let slip the wallet. It was as if a wave had snatched her babies from her hands. Her cry of pain was genuine as she watched her precious drawings being whisked away by the rapid current.

She looked up at David, who had to suppress his surprise when she hurled in fluent patois, 'My God, my wallet, I've lost my wallet! It's your fault for bringing us here! Now what?' It was a risk, but she had noted that the soldiers had accents from the north. She speculated that they would probably not know which kingdom her patois was from, never mind which region.

The soldier turned to his superior, who said: 'Search her bag; if she's a fugitive, she'll be carrying a Protestant Bible.'

The lady has her wits about her, thought Trouvier, who loosened his clasp on his knife. Jeanne handed her bag to the soldier, confident in the knowledge that he would not find her Bible due to the simple fact that she wore it on her person. It was called a chignon Bible because it was small enough for ladies to hide in their hair.

The soldier rummaged around in the sack. Then he shook his head at his superior who had been half expecting to find a bourgeoise in disguise. But Huguenot ladies are not educated to speak patois. They are bred to speak the king's French. They would not lower themselves to speak the language of peasants.

Jeanne hurled more of her patois at David about the fading light. He stood there exactly like an embarrassed husband, gormless.

'Please forgive her insolence, Sir,' he said. But the senior guard had already held up a hand, laughed out loud, and waved them on. The young guard threw Jeanne's sack to the harassed 'husband.' They then turned their horses, rode back up the shore, and cantered away. The boatman pushed on his punt.

Half an hour later, they were standing in the Duchy of Savoy. Jeanne and Claire fell into each other's arms, rejoicing for their imminent freedom from persecution.

Beneath the joy, however, Jeanne hid her grief at the loss of the precious drawings of her children.

*

By the second day's ride from Seyssel, they were easier about travelling by daylight. Now that the storm had passed, Jeanne even began to marvel at the spectacular mountainscapes, the lush alpine meadows, rocky ravines, and snow-capped crests high above.

Following the French king's example, Victor Amadeus II of Savoy had instigated a purge of Protestantism from his duchy. However, unlike their French counterparts, the Savoyard Protestants, known as Waldensians, were at least allowed to leave the dukedom if they did not wish to become Catholics overnight. Nevertheless, to avoid any unpleasant encounters with the duke's soldiers, who now had a licence to harass, David Trouvier kept his group off the beaten track.

Trouvier invariably marked the pace up front, Monsieur Lambrois kept up the rear, and Jeanne and Mademoiselle Claire rode alongside each other wherever the path permitted. Despite the fatigue from weeks of travel, and the shift to sleeping at night, the journey took on a more convivial mood. And now that they had left French soil, their conversation became less constrained, despite the guide's reminder that danger could still be lurking.

'To tell the truth, we were to wed two years ago,' said Mademoiselle Claire as she and Jeanne rode abreast along the mountain trail in the cool morning sun. 'But the Revocation put a stop to all our plans. I tried to convert, but I could not bring myself to marry before a Catholic altar.'

'So you decided to leave,' said Jeanne, who sensed the young woman's relief as she voiced her secret.

Claire simply nodded. It brought back scenes of farewell and the thought of perhaps never seeing her family again in this life. She needed an instant for the surge of emotion to subside.

Jeanne understood her agitation. She said with finality, 'You were right, my dear, to follow your conscience.'

After a moment, Claire said, 'It was Etienne who suggested we leave France; he could not bear us not being married. My dear father told the authorities I would be staying with my aunt in Bordeaux. Then we left with his blessing, though I cannot help feeling bad about it, like I'm running away.'

'You need not. You have followed your heart, and you were right,' said Jeanne. 'Listen to me: if I had left France when my husband first suggested it, we would both be together with our children now. And I would not be here today travelling without them like a lonely spinster.' Claire was pressing Jeanne's arm in sympathy when there was a movement above and then falling rubble ahead.

Two mountain men jumped down from a rock ledge with muskets at their belts. David raised a hand to halt the mules. Jeanne froze. Claire now pressed her hand to her mouth to stifle her fright as Etienne trotted up to join the guide.

'Where go you?' said one of the men, striding forward to meet them head-on. He wore a red neck scarf and a wide-brimmed hat similar to that of Trouvier.

'Geneva, if my life's worth living!' affirmed David in a raised voice. Jeanne thought it rather bold, perhaps too bold.

The guide dismounted. But then both men's faces blossomed into a broad smile as they walked into each other's arms.

'Cousin, your timing is impeccable,' said the man. David then grasped the arm of the second man—ten years younger than his cousin—in a manifestation of friendship.

Jeanne smiled her relief. Claire let out a little laugh in appreciation of the caper. Lambrois jumped down from his mule.

David introduced his cousin, Thomas Trouvier, who was accompanied by a man named Jacques, who carried a cane and wore a brown knitted cap.

'Monsieur, Mesdames, fear not. You are among friends,' said Thomas. He then explained to the group that on this day, the Lord's Day, they were lookouts. For what, the party would soon hear and see for themselves.

The man named Jacques, a taciturn shepherd in his thirties, led them on. Towing his mule, David walked beside Thomas while exchanging news of high waters and impending snowfalls. Jeanne, Claire, and Etienne Lambrois followed on mule-back.

After a five-minute trek, they veered off the mountain path. Everyone dismounted to avoid the low branches. In a moment, they could hear singing. Then the rocky path developed into a clearing fringed by spindly spruce trees, and they were met with the heartening sight of a congregation of Waldensians who had just broken into beautiful song. Jeanne recognised the song 'Through the Desert of My Suffering.'

The preacher was standing on wooden steps. The congregation of about sixty souls of every age and condition was standing, kneeling, or sitting on rocks all around, like the first Christians persecuted by Romans, thought Jeanne. Today, however, it was Roman Catholics who were the persecutors. Clandestine services in the hills like this one were held throughout Savoy for Protestants no longer allowed to practice their faith in their villages.

Jeanne let fall the rein of her mule and walked into the assembly. She knelt down, and a feeling of rejuvenation inhabited her. It was as if a great burden were being lifted from her back as she thanked Christ for helping her keep her faith.

Claire and Etienne exchanged a loving smile, advanced together, then knelt beside Jeanne and joined in the last couplets of the song.

It assuaged the pain in Jeanne's heart to feel her warm tears stream down her cold cheeks as she prayed to God for her husband and her children. She resolved there and then that once she arrived in Geneva, she would spend the remainder of her money, if necessary, to bring at least Elizabeth to her side. Elizabeth was old enough to stand up to the rigours of the long and perilous journey. That was what she would do once she got to Geneva.

*

They passed over the drawbridge the following day, and entered through the south city gate, recently fortified. Labourers and builders on scaffolds were finishing reinforcement work along the stone ramparts.

Trouvier led his party on through the tall interior gate, porte de la Tartace, then to the lower city centre. The colourful hullabaloo of the bustling market with its savoury smells and unashamed abundance was a heartening sight indeed. People knew instinctively whence they had come, and as they filled their gourdes with water at a fountain, some folk doffed their hats in a sign of welcome, while a few others stared with curiosity, or was it disapproval?

Having stabled their mules, a short time later, they pushed the heavy door of a tavern, where they ordered food and sent a messenger to inform their contacts of their arrival. Soon, Claire and her cabinetmaker were met by the relative who had offered them board and lodging until they were properly married and settled. Jeanne was glad to see he was a very civil man, middle-aged and soberly dressed. Of course Jeanne would see them again; of course they would sit together in church. Etienne Lambrois and his bride-to-be took their leave in an effusion of thanks to both their guide and Madame Delpech.

The log fire crackled in the hearth. A dog sat scratching itself by their table, then yawned. Now alone with Trouvier, Jeanne seized the moment to ask him if he would bring her one of her children from Montauban. But the guide, whose usual job was shearing and shepherding, had thought a lot since the river episode in Seyssel. He had got out of a tricky spot, partly, it was true, thanks to Jeanne. But the fact remained that he had been close to either being arrested or committing murder. Both notions made him feel uncomfortable. His luck had held out until now, so maybe he ought not to push it any further. Besides, he had already made a handsome stash of money, much more than he could have earned in many years of herding and shearing sheep, and he hoped to be around long enough to enjoy it, maybe get himself a place of his own. He was not without sympathy for the lady, who was desperate to recover some of her children. But as a matter of principle, he tried never to get involved; it was a question of self-preservation. After all, it was his head that would be on the block should he get caught. He told her he could not.

A neatly dressed gentleman walked into the tavern, where people were drinking ale and smoking wooden pipes. He had a well-trimmed beard, and wore a dark tunic and white cloth collar under a black cloak. He scanned the noisy room twice before his eyes fell again upon a country woman with her flank to him. She was wearing a peasant woman's white bonnet and was deep in conversation with a man of rustic appearance. Could that possibly be Jeanne Delpech de Castanet? Surely not. Yet the poise of her head compelled him to walk over to the table, where earthen bowls of stew and wooden tankards of ale had been served. He had a difficult task.

Trouvier looked up on the approach of the gentleman, who doffed his felt hat, revealing his thinning grey hair. Jeanne turned to face him.

'Madame Delpech? Thank God you have arrived safely.'

She instantly recognised Samuel Duvaux, the former pastor of Montauban who had left France three years before the Revocation. He had aged but had retained his benevolent smile. After the introductions, he pulled up a stool to take the weight off his feet. He explained he had been expecting her.

'Indeed, I received another note from your dear sister,' said the pastor, who immediately regretted mentioning Suzanne's letter. He adroitly steered conversation into another direction. 'I thought you would be here last week, actually, and was beginning to worry. But your room is made up, and you must know, as a refugee, you are officially welcome to winter in Geneva until April, although if you need to stay longer, I am sure we shall be able to sort something out.' But his uncharacteristic quick succession of pleasantries did not go unnoticed by Jeanne.

She said, 'Thank you so much. What news has my sister?' The pastor's delayed response, and his expression that became more solemn, told her all was not well. 'Something is wrong,' Jeanne said, 'isn't there?'

'My dear lady, I fear this is perhaps not the place . . .'

'Tell me, please,' she said. She was prepared for Jacob's passing, had been for so long. It would almost come as a relief, for it would perhaps mean she would no longer have nightmares of him being tortured.

Pastor Duvaux touched her arm and said, 'Your daughter. Louise.'

He did not need to say any more. Jeanne remained silent, dignified in her grief.

That evening, the soft bed and clean linen gave comfort to her body but no consolation to her mind. Her eyes were red and her face swollen from silently mourning the death of her daughter.

She reread the letter written by the hand of Suzanne. There was no signature, no mention of names either. It was a precautionary practice that gave protection in case the document got into the wrong hands. It told her that it was a fever that had taken her child away. The nurse said she had been playing near the latrines. She always was such an inquisitive child. Jeanne wrapped her arms around her belly, brought her knees up to the foetal position as she realised she would never be able to visit her child's grave. Could all this hardship have been for nothing? Was there no end to it?

Then she remembered that Jesus had said, 'Let the little children come to me.' She fell asleep.

*

Three days had passed since Jeanne's first night in Geneva.

The thin layer of snow that fell during the night had melted by morning. A little before noon, Monsieur Trouvier was shown into the pastor's parlour. He got to his feet when Jeanne entered. She had given up her peasant garb for a simple dress and shawl. Trouvier noticed she looked refreshed but pale. Jeanne noticed how much her guide looked out of place in the simple but elegant sitting room. She well knew what an astute man he was, and what mettle he was made of. And yet, standing there in his boots, holding his grubby hat, he looked more rural than ever, almost uncivilised. This was how she would have seen him before her hardships began. But now she knew different. Her struggles had made her a better person, she thought to herself. She smiled and sat down on the edge of an armchair.

She said, 'Thank you for your visit, Monsieur Trouvier. Please take a seat.'

'I've been thinking,' said the guide as he took a pew on the chair opposite. 'I'll go for you. I can bring back one of your children. Only one.'

'Thank you, thank you,' said Jeanne, holding her hands together.

'But you do realise that a young child under ten, unused to the wilds, might not survive the journey?'

'Yes, I have thought about that. Elizabeth shall go with you. She is thirteen years old.'

'Thirteen is good. All right, then. Though there is the added danger of winter. Although on the other hand, I s'pose the cold nights will keep the patrols away.'

13

December 1687 to February 1688

TWO MONTHS QUICKLY passed, during which Jeanne discovered she could earn a modest living from weaving.

She had used the best part of her remaining money to purchase a small loom. Church acquaintances tried to persuade her that artisan work was below her. But she would not accept charity from the refugee relief fund, and only continued staying at the pastor's residence because of his gentle insistence. Her clientele grew, thanks to the church, and to the reputation of Huguenot weavers whose techniques she had learnt from Monsieur Cordelle.

She had lost everything. She no longer cared for material things, so she found she could live on very little and put coin aside for when she would no longer just have her own upkeep to pay for. She looked forward to one day soon being reunited with her eldest daughter. Any spare time was used making for Elizabeth a set of winter clothes which she could alter accordingly when she saw her. Jeanne often wondered what she was like now. A proper little madam, knowing Lizzy.

Every day, she thanked the Lord for placing in her path

a weaver and a shepherd, and considered how the humblest in society had given her self-sufficiency and filled her with hope to carry on.

A week before Christmastide, she received a note. Judging from the untutored handwriting, it could only be from Trouvier. She tore it open with trembling hands. It read: '*Your little lady wishes to stay with her friends. She refuses to leave her home town. I cannot wait anymore. I am very sorry.*'

*

January in Geneva was colder than anything Jeanne had ever experienced.

In the last week of that month, the lake froze around the port. Trees crystallised into fantastic ice sculptures, children played in snowdrifts heaped up by the north wind, and icicles formed under cornices of tall buildings that lined the steep streets leading up to the upper town and Protestant cathedral.

However, the lengthening days meant that Jeanne was able to work longer hours at her loom. The act of producing fabric, something physically useful, not only allowed her to earn a modest living, it kept her mind focused on creation rather than her own ruin. It also saved her from lingering in hope of a letter from Suzanne that never came. She deduced her sister's correspondence somehow must have been intercepted, unless there was another reason for the lack of tidings.

Of course there were times when she could not keep her mind from exploring ways of returning to Montauban to retrieve her children herself. She had not seen them for nigh on two years. However, those deliberations that sometimes came to frustrate her were quickly quashed by her economic reality. She simply had no more means to hire a guide.

But more than this, the extra daylight hours allowed her to invest herself further in her new occupation.

She was now living in third-floor rooms above a bakery that was situated on Place du Molard, a busy marketplace of the lower town that opened onto the lake harbour on the north side. She had wanted to be able to live through her sufferance in her own space, where she could choose to eat, sleep, work, and sometimes cry, as she pleased.

Pastor Duvaux had been supportive about the move. Together, they had found the rooms, which were well-heated thanks to the baker's oven, and she frankly did not mind the early-morning noise. On the contrary, it brought her comfort to hear the bakery in action and the daily rituals of family life going on beneath her.

She did, however, and gladly so, agree to retain her seat at the pastor's table every Sunday after church. Jeanne found the conversation during these meals helped her better understand Genevese society. And it was during one of these meals that she discovered her new raison d'être.

Jeanne was sitting at the end of the table in her usual place nearest the tiled stove, the place once occupied by the pastor's deceased wife. When a lady once pointed this out to her, at first Jeanne felt slightly awkward about it. But then her practical sense quelled any feelings of impropriety. The pastor's wife was dead, and she was cold, so that was where she continued to sit.

To her right sat the deacon, a wiry man with a full head of white hair. Next to him were Madame and Monsieur Tagliani, the latter a respected merchant and member of the

Council of Two Hundred. The pastor presided at the opposite end of the table, and to his right sat the guests of honour, Monsieur Ezéchiel Gallatin and his wife. Gallatin was one of the four syndics elected to form the executive government of the Republic of Geneva. Jeanne noticed the dishes were well- garnished. She wondered if this was owing to the importance of the guests or to the extent of Monsieur the Syndic's prodigious belly. At any rate, the pastor was pulling out all the stops of the organ to get his special guest to rally to his cause.

Both she and the pastor had wanted to question him about the plight of Protestant refugees who would undoubtedly continue to flow into Geneva at a greater rate come spring.

'I really do not know how much longer we can open our gates to everyone,' said the syndic, who then shovelled a chunk of capon into his mouth using a fork, an unmanly utensil that he had nonetheless learnt to tame on diplomatic missions to Paris.

'With all due respect, Monsieur the Syndic,' said the pastor, chuckling cordially. 'May I remind us all what has in the past bolstered our economy and made our little city prosperous?'

'*I* certainly need no reminding,' said Monsieur Tagliani, seeing as Monsieur the Syndic had his face full. 'Protestant refugees during the governance of Jean Calvin. And I am proud to say that at least one of my forebears on my mother's side was among them.'

'Quite, quite,' said the syndic. 'And my great-great-great-great-grandfather was a clockmaker from Paris, as you well know. But come, Pastor Duvaux, that is beside the question.'

173

'Then what is the question, Monsieur the Syndic?' said Jeanne, with something of her sister's affable musicality. Dinners with her husband and his clients had taught her that a contestation always had a better chance of hitting home when said with a smile.

'The question is, dear Madame,' returned the syndic, turning his head to gradually encompass the whole table. 'Where are we going to put them all? That is the question!' He gave a fine twirl of his fork, then brought it back to his mouth.

The pastor said, 'I realise that the relief fund is not inexhaustible; however, many of the refugees have means to rent or to acquire lodgings.'

Jeanne added, 'At the least, most of them have skills which will allow them to establish and sustain themselves in the long run.'

The pastor continued, 'Indeed, and those with means will inevitably create work. But if the local workforce cannot meet the demand, then such affluent individuals will move on to enrich Brandenburg and Holland instead.'

Monsieur Tagliani said, 'Put like that, I admit it does make sense for the town to grasp this opportunity as it did under Calvin. And I do not care if the French king's diplomat wants us to move them on.'

'You mean Monsieur Dupré. I confess, I am not overly keen on his manners either,' said the syndic, which gave some relief to Jeanne and Pastor Duvaux.

Otherwise known as the Résident de France, Monsieur Dupré was responsible for conveying to the Genevan authorities Louis XIV's desire to rid Geneva of Huguenots. Some high-ranking officials were beginning to fear a French invasion if the small Protestant republic did not comply.

As the syndic washed down his food with a quaff of wine, Madame Tagliani, a mouse of a woman but with a certain pedigree, took advantage of the short silence to add her reasoning. She said, 'Makes me wonder if the king of France realises what a generous windfall he is giving to his rivals.'

'Well said, Madame,' said Jeanne, who was thinking exactly the same thing.

Indeed, during the short time Jeanne Delpech had been in Geneva, the pews of Saint Germain's church had swelled with tanners, shearers, lawyers, labourers, clockmakers, physicians, weavers, and more. No wonder King Louis had made up laws to prevent them from leaving his kingdom. The loss of income from taxes would be considerable, not to mention the drain of talent. That being said, to a certain extent, other laws shrewdly made up for the shortfall by allowing the king to confiscate the fortunes of wealthy Protestants who were sent to the galleys.

But Madame Tagliani was right. For the state capable of harnessing such an inflow of expertise, it was surely a windfall, even if not all Swiss cantons saw it that way. Indeed, the fact was, some of them were encouraging escapees to continue their path northward to the more accommodating pastures of Prussia and Holland.

The deacon, a sensible, calculating man and ageing bachelor, said, 'But the problem remains. Those without means will need time and shelter before they can stand on their own two feet. Or would you rather have them camp outside the city walls?'

'Certainly not,' said the syndic, 'it would look messy.'

It suddenly occurred to Jeanne that a role was waiting to

be filled, and filled by her. She had been so centred on her own misgivings that she had not seen what must surely be the reason God had brought her to this cold refuge, pretty as it was. It now all made sense: she had come to serve her persecuted brethren.

She stood up, dropped the facade of affability, and with unshakable conviction, she said, 'Already these people are pushed away in Savoy and some Swiss cantons. We cannot push them away from the very capital of Protestantism, the city of Jean Calvin, the defender of the Reform, and our spiritual leader! We shall call upon the goodness of people's hearts. And I shall take care of finding the extra space required.'

There was no objection to that. On the contrary, the syndic let out a belch of approval. The pastor and the deacon gave her a doting smile, as if their prayers had been answered. She would in effect be removing a thorn from their side, what with the deacon lacking experience with the fairer sex and the pastor no longer able to call on his wife on account of her being dead.

What was more, Madame Delpech had first-hand experience as a refugee. She had a certain standing, possessed the gift of being able to speak with anyone of any social rank, and had become an active and respected member of Saint Germain's church. And of course, most of all, she knew about the secrets of womankind and motherhood.

Jeanne sat back down amid encouraging interjections, while the whole table clapped their hands.

Her first task would be to garner a list of addresses from churchgoers, where refugees could find a bed and a warm meal until they got settled or continued north.

*

Come February, Jeanne noticed a steady rise in the number of newcomers arriving through the city gates. Once again, the refugee issue was the main topic of conversation in the Genevese marketplace. The authorities were beginning to realise the amplitude of the situation and willingly directed refugees to organisations where they could find assistance.

Weaving on her loom one February morning, her thoughts turned to the grateful young couple—the wife with a baby in her belly—whom she had placed the day before with a church acquaintance.

The patter of footsteps followed by a knock on the door brought her out of her contemplation, and told her it was getting on for noon. Every day, little Denise, the baker's daughter, aged seven and very proper, delivered Jeanne's bread, for which the baker and his wife refused payment. It was their way of supporting the refugees, and hopefully kept Madame Delpech from asking if they could put up a foreigner. Jeanne finished passing the shuttle across the weft, squeezed the warp with the beater, and went to open the door.

'Oh, thank you, Denise, my sweet,' she said to the little girl, who stood in the doorway with a galette of bread and a gummy smile. 'And how are we this morning? Let me see your tooth.'

The child handed over the bread and showed her two gaps where the bottom front teeth had been.

'Well, well, what have we here, a little rabbit who has lost her teeth?'

'Oh no, Madame, not a rabbit,' said the child, who frowned at the thought of being compared to her grandma's favourite dish, a *civet de lapin*.

'Ah, but a pretty little rabbit, though,' Jeanne continued, and the child's frown turned into a polite smile. Of course, the lady was not expected to know about rabbit stew, even less about her grandma's delight in sucking rabbits' heads.

It struck Jeanne that Isabelle would have all her teeth by now, that she would have suffered teething without the love and patience of a mother. Jeanne had learnt to live with these impromptu flashes which popped into her head at any time of the day, during any activity or event.

She shook the anxiety from her mind as footsteps on the narrow wooden staircase announced another visitor. She recognised the constant and deliberate footfall of Pastor Duvaux.

'Off you run, my angel,' she said to Denise. The child ran off, passing the pastor as he came upon the landing.

'My dear Madame Delpech, I am sorry,' he said, doffing his hat as he arrived at the door. 'We have a father and a son this time. I was out when they called, but they left a message. And they asked for you. Your name knows no bounds, my dear. They are waiting at the tavern.'

Her new role, which had enabled her to recover some shreds of self-respect, had come as a blessing to the pastor. He now systematically passed onto her the charge of organising accommodation, food, and other requisites necessary for children, not to mention the female condition. This role he would have delegated to his wife, had she still been alive. Jeanne was careful not to let any misunderstanding creep into their relationship.

'Then please step inside, Pastor Duvaux, while I put on my coat,' said Jeanne, who crossed the room to her small bedroom. 'I shall be with you in a moment.'

With the increase of asylum seekers, the pastor was calling more often than before, to the extent of her having to delay some of her textile orders. But it was for the right cause, and it was bringing her attention and paradoxically more customers.

A few minutes later, she was standing before him, clad in her outdoor garments with a hat firmly pinned to her head and a heavy woollen shawl wrapped around her shoulders.

'You might have to take them in for just one night until I check if the captain's lodgers have vacated their room yet,' said Jeanne as they stepped out into the freezing street. She continued, 'A carpenter, his wife, and their children from Aigues-Mortes. They have found somewhere down by the river near the mills, a bit damp, but I believe it meets their requirements.'

'Yes, of course, whatever you say,' said the pastor.

The square was still bustling with shoppers, and barrows, baskets, and stalls whose vendors were stamping their feet and clapping half-mittened hands. The day was crisp: an icy chill swept off Lake Geneva, and horses and beasts of burden moved in shrouds of vapour that escaped from their muzzles. Jeanne and the pastor quickly wended through the busy lower town, past Madeleine church, where they bumped into acquaintances with whom they exchanged polite salutations, and into a wide, cobbled lane.

'I hope the syndic will see reason,' said Jeanne. 'We need his support for more temporary accommodation.'

'I hope so too,' said the pastor. 'I fear that, with the spring, the numbers will increase more quickly than we thought. It will be a difficult job to accommodate everyone. Thank goodness you have come to help, dear Madame

Delpech.' Jeanne gave a modest smile but hurried her step. However, her quickened pace did not stop his train of thought, and he said, 'You are, if I may say, a perfect . . . godsend!'

She had heard him say it before but was nonetheless flattered, though she made every effort to appear unmoved. She did not want to give him the wrong impression. Moreover, she noticed something new in the pastor's eyes that gave her a secret cause for alarm, and something more dramatic, too, in his speech, which had faltered uncharacteristically on the last syllables. Was the pastor falling in love? She shut out the notion from her mind as they arrived at their destination.

'Here we are,' he said, opening the sturdy wooden door for her. She then let him lead the way into the warm and smoky tavern.

They had entered the spacious room together many times over the past month, always for the same reason, and each time, the pastor had to overcome his natural reticence. Such places were often the refuge of corruption and vice, rarely visited by men of the cloth. However, given the present crisis, his presence was tolerated as long as his visit was short and he did not preach.

Jeanne had become familiar with the setting, which she found demystifying and which she would surely not have otherwise known in her life: the nonchalant dog, the blazing fire, the banter of patrons over a table scattered with playing cards, and the blended smells of ale, pipe smoke, and broth. A great iron cauldron sat permanently on the stove and was constantly topped up in the morning with meat, carrots, cabbage, onion, and dregs of red wine, all peppered with spices and herbs. She remembered how very good and heartening it was, especially after a long and exhausting trek. And every time she entered the place, she still felt the sense of comfort of that first time, when she had looked up and seen the pastor's benevolent smile.

Whatever her frame of mind, whatever her private sufferance, she always made a point of reserving the same welcome even when the stranger's face did not seem to register it. Nobody knew the inner battles a person was going through, the torments a person had already endured, and she would at least try to radiate a feeling of friendship while keeping a respectful distance. She knew as well as anyone how harrowing and confusing it was to be scornfully rejected in one land and find welcome in another.

As per their habit, they looked towards the barman, a middle-aged and barrel-shaped man with rugged features. He had a gash from his left cheek to his lip which gave him a grim rictus, a remnant of his soldiering days. But for all his roughness, he had heart; Jeanne sensed it.

She had become a familiar face to him now. He noted she was never ostentatious or pompous to the foreigners; she was never haughty or overbearing. He liked her for that, and appreciated her for sensing the kindness in his own soul.

He lifted his eyes, and jerked his head towards the table nearest the fire where the father and son were sitting in front of bowls of stew and a *quignon* of bread. The pastor and the lady directed their course towards them.

It was often the case during these times of religious persecution that young men would give a pretext for a visit to a distant French town for work, leaving the father with the mother to take care of the family business at home. In this way, the family heritage was not given up to the king's treasury, and the offspring would have the means to start a new life in a Protestant country without being missed.

But in the present case, the arrival of both son and father could only mean that the man must have lost his wife. And Jeanne could now see that the son, who had his back to her, was just a boy.

Halfway across the room, she had an awful premonition that shook her confidence. The man sitting in front of the lad looked up. It was Trouvier, the guide whom she had paid and on whom she had counted to bring her daughter to her.

A realisation struck.

'Oh, my God!' She held her hand over her mouth. The boy had looked around to face her.

The pastor stepped out of her path as she rushed forward to meet Paul. She let go of all restraint, hot tears streaming down her face.

'My son, my beautiful boy!' she cried as the young lad, now nearly as tall as she was, pushed back his stool, stood up with arms open wide, and then buried his cheek into his mother's bosom.

'Mama, Mama, dear Mama, I am here now,' he said.

VOYAGE OF MALICE

Book 2 of the Huguenot Connection trilogy is available
now from Amazon and all major high street bookstores

VOYAGE OF MALICE

Book 2 of the Huguenot Connection trilogy

Excerpt

ONE

FROM THE FOREMOST cabin of *La Marie*, Jacob Delpech steadied himself as best he could against the brine-splashed frame of the porthole. He stooped to avoid hitting his head on the coarse timber beam, so low was the cabin where he and his Huguenot brethren were incarcerated. But the view was certainly worth the effort, he thought, as the French pink, a three-masted cargo ship, pitched and rolled into the Bay of Cadiz.

'So this is the gateway to the ocean sea,' he said, almost to himself.

Mademoiselle Marianne Duvivier, standing next to him, made a comment on the pageant of colour growing nearer and bigger. Indeed, the Spanish port's importance was attested by the multitude of foreign merchant ships anchored here and there, flying their colours atop their main masts.

It occurred to Jacob that they were now only one stop away from their Caribbean island prison. That is, provided the ship, more apt for coastal ferrying than sailing the great sea, did not turn turtle en route—for she bobbed like a barrel.

The passage from Gibraltar, though short, had been rough enough to shake up the stomachs of the hardiest of seafarers. In fact it had finished off two prisoners in the cabin next door, which housed galley slaves too old or too infirm for service. However, miraculously perhaps, the eighty or so Protestant prisoners were none the worse for wear despite being at the bow of the ship, that part which took the full brunt of the waves. But unlike the poor lame wretches next door, at least they bore no visible chains. And most of the Huguenot men and women seemed to be gaining their sea legs at last.

To Marianne Duvivier's great relief, they could now spy *La Concorde*, the great ship that had accompanied them much of the way from Marseille, and which carried a greater load of galley slave labour and Huguenot prisoners. More efficient and faster than *La Marie*, she had sailed ahead from Gibraltar and was already at anchor in the ancient Andalusian harbour. Significantly larger and built for the high seas, she was also more stable and seemed to sit in the port waters like an albatross among chicks, hardly bobbing amid the ripples.

La Marie dropped her anchors just a gunshot from *La Concorde*, but not close enough for prisoners to exchange words, nor parallel so that they could see each other. Nevertheless, Marianne Duvivier was still standing at the gun port an hour after their arrival, hoping for her grandmother to show her head through a porthole of the great ship.

She turned to Jacob, who had joined her again. In her resolute and selfless way, she said, 'I am so glad it was my grandmother and not I who was sent aboard the *Concorde*.' She was referring to the cruel separation from Madame de Fontenay at the embarkation point in Marseille. Jacob had since fathomed that separating grandmother and granddaughter was certainly a ploy between guards so that the girl could be more easily singled out and plucked from the crowd. However, her ravisher had ended up drowning with the first mate and another seaman when the longboat he was rowing capsized in the port of Toulon, the day after his failed abduction. And by a strange twist of fate, or Providence maybe, his death had granted her protection, for sailors were deeply superstitious.

'Yes, quite,' said Jacob, nodding towards the Spanish quay. 'Otherwise she may have been leaving the ship earlier than planned.'

The girl followed his eyes to where the dead prisoners, bound in hessian sacks, were being hoisted to quay from the longboat, then unceremoniously dumped like dead pigs onto a barrow. It was still early morning. The harbour was just beginning to stir in the grey light, and they could clearly hear the vociferations in French and Spanish about the stench emanating from the bodies. The Spaniard made several signs of the cross before taking up the shafts of the barrow, then wheeled the dead men away to God-knows-where.

Delpech felt a pang of injustice for the galley slave, whom he had known to have been a God-fearing shoemaker whose only crime had been the illicit purchase of salt. His wife and children would not even be able to mourn his passing properly without the body, he thought. He inwardly prayed for the man's soul to accept a place in heaven, if it so pleased God.

'I would willingly miss three days' worth of rations for a place on board the Concorde,' said one white-haired gentleman, a surgeon named Emile Bourget.

'Can't say you would be missing much,' said Madame Fesquet, the middle-aged matron who had comforted Marianne after the attempted abduction.

'Let us not allow our regrets to undermine us, my dear Professor,' said Jacob, touching the man's arm. 'Instead let us spend our effort seeking God's grace in our misfortune.'

'Yes, you are right, Sir,' said Bourget. 'Forgive me my weakness.'

Madame Fesquet, in her matronly way, said, 'Praise be to God that we have arrived safely and have been granted this reprieve from the treacherous sea!'

Jacob thought she needn't be so loud; she might rouse the guards. But he bowed his head and said *Amen* anyway. After all, she was of goodwill and was only voicing her support of his remark.

Delpech had inadvertently become something of a moral touchstone among even these adamantly virtuous people. He had become their spokesman whenever their meagre rights of humanity needed to be reaffirmed to the captain, even though these demands were always made through the guards. The unsolicited honour no doubt had something to do with his forthright eloquence, his former position and fortune, and perhaps most of all, his standing up to the sailor who had one night tried to ravish the girl from the cabin.

Yet in truth, all Jacob Delpech really wanted was to lie

low and get through this nightmare until he could find a way to escape the madness. And, with God's help, recover his wife and children.

The Huguenot ladies and gentlemen agreed to take advantage of the month-long stop in the Spanish port to swab the planks of their cabin, and to reduce the number of vermin. But undertaking the former required water and cloths, at the very least.

Jacob bravely accepted the task of go-between. He decided, however, to wait for the most appropriate moment when the soil buckets had been emptied, and when the least volatile guard came on duty. So it was not until after their noon slops—a mix of pellet-like peas and half-boiled fish—that he was able to put the question to the guard through the iron slats of the half-timbered door.

GUARD: What now?

DELPECH: We desire to speak to the captain.

GUARD: Cap'ain's busy.

DELPECH: It is a matter of hygiene.

GUARD: Don't care what it's about, mate, I said he's busy. And when he's busy, it means he don't wanna be disturbed, savvy?

DELPECH: Then would you please be so kind as to ask him if we may be supplied with extra buckets and some rope so that we can haul seawater into the cabin.

GUARD: So you can escape more like, cheeky bugger!

DELPECH: Not at all. We would simply like to clean the cabin.

GUARD: I'll give you a bucket, all right, a bucket of heretic shit if you don't watch out!

DELPECH: Then would you kindly supply us with the water yourselves? And some sackcloth? I pray that you put my demand to the captain, or at least to the first mate, should the captain be unavailable. Will you do that?

GUARD: Pwah. All right, but woe betide you if I get my arse kicked!

Jacob Delpech had become as inured to threats as he had to the revolting stench of the cabin, full of unwashed people and buckets of excrement. Over the past two years, from one prison to another, he had been threatened with hanging, perishing in damnation, being burnt alive at the stake, having his balls stuffed into his mouth, and finally, being sent to America. Only the last threat had so far been carried out, which enabled him to take the guard's colourful language with a pinch of salt, and to pursue his demands calmly and collectedly.

An hour went by before the key clunked in the lock.

'Where's the prat who asked for water?' said the guard, peeking through the iron slats of the door.

'I am the one who asked for water. And rope,' said Jacob, who was still by the door, imperturbable.

'It's your lucky day, pal. The captain sends his blessings!'

The door was flung open, and three men with malicious grins stood in the doorway, each holding a pail. Delpech instinctively held up his hands to shield his head as three columns of water drenched him and those immediately around him from head to foot. The men laughed out loud. Then the guard pulled the heavy door shut and turned the key in the lock.

Jacob prayed inwardly for the strength to continue to

suffer humiliation, torture, and even death for his faith. However, at least the guard's threat was only partially carried out. Thankfully, seawater was all that was in the buckets.

Nevertheless, to state that Delpech was becoming weary of the crew's scorn—scorn that he suspected was fuelled by a callous captain—was an understatement. But he kept it to himself, and prayed the day would come when he could escape to carry out his plan.

*

Captain Joseph Reners, thirty-nine, was a merchant. A strong leader and very proud of his person, he was as able with low life as he was with the elite, and he enjoyed the company in both the Old World and the New. He loved his occupation, buying and selling, which took him to places where a man could forget himself. What he disliked, though, were the bits in-between, the seafaring bits which were either extremely dangerous or downright boring.

He vaunted himself as being well travelled and delighted in thrilling the bourgeoisie in Cadiz, especially the ladies, with tales of peril at sea and man-eating savages called cannibals. Given his gregarious nature, he had acquired expert knowledge of parlour games and card playing. In short, he lived for the social life on land, and this latest venture transporting galley slaves and Huguenots gave him the means to indulge wholeheartedly in his passions, from Cadiz to the Spanish Main. Nevertheless, over the years he had traced a regular circuit and by consequence had a reputation to keep up, at least in Europe, if he were not to be shunned by his usual hosts.

Consequently, a day after the water-throwing incident,

the crew's degree of crassness towards their prisoners slipped down a few notches, and their attitude became, if not respectful, at least more tolerable. The soil buckets were emptied before they were completely full, and the peas were cooked, so they no longer ended up in those buckets. The salted beef, however, remained as tough as boot leather, and the cold fish still resembled a kind of briny porridge. But most of all, the Huguenot detainees no longer ran the risk of being drenched by buckets of seawater whenever they knelt down to pray.

Jacob correctly supposed that this change was owing to the captain's desire to show a façade of respectability and humanity during his stay in the Spanish port town.

What is more, the shift in behaviour was sustained and even enhanced, thanks to a series of visits paid to the Huguenots during their stopover.

Dutch and English Protestant merchants who had settled in the Iberian port quickly got wind of the 'cargo' of Huguenots. It had become a normal occurrence to hear of lame slaves being transported to the New World. But how could respectable, devout Christians be stripped of their earthly possessions and dispelled from their homeland for simply remaining faithful to their religious conscience?

Despite Louis XIV's attempt to draw a veil over his religious purge and conceal it from the outside world, word had nevertheless percolated out of France. Tens of thousands of Huguenot escapees had taken with them to Geneva, Bearn, Brandenburg, Saxony, Amsterdam, and London tales of unfair trials, family separations, enslavement, and incarceration. French etiquette was quickly going out of fashion. It was losing its capacity to charm the breaches off the European bourgeoisie as the darker side of the Sun King was becoming apparent. And here in Cadiz was the chance to see the living proof.

The captains of neither *La Marie* nor *La Concorde* did anything to prevent visits to their ships. On the contrary, Reners for one was astute enough to give orders not to impede such visits, as proof that he himself had nothing to hide, that he was only carrying out the King's orders. When asked at his hosts' table about his cargo of Huguenots, he would make a point of stating that the poor wretches on his ship were treated with humanity, even allowed to pray to their God, in spite of their disloyalty to their King.

On the morning of 22 October 1687, the second morning after the French ships' arrival, Mr Izaäk van der Veen and his wife were the first of the Protestant merchants to visit *La Marie*. The Dutchman was an influential broker with links to counters in Holland and the West Indies. He had done business with the captain on numerous occasions, usually for the purchase of barrels of French wine which went down well with the multi-cultured population of Cadiz, as well as his Flemish buyers.

Mrs van der Veen, a straight-faced and well-endowed lady with mothering hips, climbed aboard *La Marie*, taking care not to dirty her dress in the rigging. The Dutchman knew the ship from previous visits, although this time neither he nor his wife was there to choose barrels of beverage. This was just as well, as the space normally given over to wine and spirits had been converted for the captain's human cargo.

Both Mr and Mrs van der Veen were dressed with sobriety in accordance with their reformist beliefs. They were greeted by the second in command. This did not disgruntle the visitors in the slightest, as they knew of the captain's legendary distaste for dwelling on board his ship. The remaining crew were busy offloading cargo destined for Cadiz. The visiting couple advanced carefully to avoid slipping on the wet decking, and continued past sailors swabbing the main deck.

Mr van der Veen followed the second mate down the scuttle hatch into the tween deck, and then turned to assist his wife. She immediately noticed that the open space that once spanned from the capstan to the windlass was now partitioned off into cabins. And thank goodness she had thought to perfume her handkerchief, which she now held to her nose. The savoury and sickly smell of food, urine, tar, and dank timber grew stronger as they advanced towards the galley slave cabin, where a large rat stood nibbling at a flat square of flesh—a prize stolen from an inmate's bowl. The rat had grasped that a man inside the cabin who carelessly placed his bowl on the ground had no chance of catching the rodent once it had scooted with the food under the door. But on the approach of the intruders, the hideous creature showed its teeth, jealously took up its prize, and indignantly scampered away.

Mrs van der Veen and her husband turned to each other with a look which said they were dreading to see the conditions in which their brothers and sisters in faith were being held captive.

Then the sound of a woman's voice rose up in song. It was spontaneously joined by a host of male and female voices, and the Dutch lady recognised a psalm that sounded beautiful, sung in the French language.

They hastened their step to the Huguenots' cell and stood to watch through the iron slats. The inmates nearest the door stopped their song, and for a suspended moment stood watching the couple staring back at them.

Mrs Van der Veen, who spoke some French, had prepared her introductory sentence in her head that morning. But it did not come out, so absorbed was she by the piteous sight of the scene before her. Instead she put her hands together in prayer. Her husband followed suit. Then gradually, like a wave leading from the door, the Huguenots also stood or knelt in silent prayer.

At last, the Dutch couple looked up, and their eyes met those of a slim gentleman with cropped hair who took a step from the crowd.

'Madame,' he said in French. 'Do not pity us but rather our persecutors. For we are the privileged few whom the Lord has graced with the chance to earn a place in heaven. There is no need to shed your tears for us.'

'Monsieur, please forgive us,' said Mrs Van der Veen. 'We were not prepared to see such injustice before our very eyes.'

The second mate who had accompanied them was standing sheepishly with the guard, three paces back. Mr van der Veen turned to them and asked in Spanish to open the door so that he and his wife could enter the cell. The second mate gave the nod to the guard, who opened the door, then locked it behind them.

The gaunt-looking man with the cropped head introduced himself. 'I am Jacob Delpech de Castanet,' he said. Other men and women huddled around them without thronging, and introduced themselves in the gentlest manner.

'Dear lady, your heart is noble and kind,' said one young lady who introduced herself as Mademoiselle Duvivier. 'But please do not be afraid to hold your handkerchief to your nose. We understand that the odours must be intolerable to someone unused to this despicable den.'

'Thank you for your consideration,' said Mrs Van der Veen, 'but allow me the honour of sharing a part of your humiliation and sufferance with you. It will make me nobler.'

Mr van der Veen said slowly in Spanish, 'If we can bring you any comfort at all, we shall be eternally grateful.'

Mrs van der Veen said in French, 'I shall bring you vials of perfume, which will at least sweeten the air around you, as well as other provisions. Please tell us what you need most.'

'You are kind, my good lady,' said one Huguenot woman.

'A splendid idea,' said Madame Fesquet. 'It will distance the bad smells that breed disease.'

Mademoiselle Duvivier said, 'The disease is also brought by the vermin, I fear. As Jesus tells us to travel through life in a clean body, we should very much like to embark on our voyage in a clean cabin.'

'We have been enclosed in this cabin for the past four weeks,' said Jacob. 'Alas, in spite of our demands, we are deprived of water and rags for swabbing.'

'I will ask the captain to see to it that you are equipped,' said Mr van de Veen, who then let his wife translate.

*

By the following morning, not only was the Huguenots' wish for water and cloth granted, but more visits followed from other Dutch and English contingents, and continued throughout the

Huguenots' stay in Cadiz harbour. Each visit uplifted their spirits, like a rag of blue sky in an otherwise murky firmament. They saw each visit as a ray of God's love that galvanised their faith and filled their souls with new courage. It meant He had not abandoned them. Now they could embark on the long, perilous voyage across the great sea, secure in the knowledge that their place in heaven was assured. What, after all, was earthly suffering compared to eternal life?

The visiting parties also brought very earthly provisions: dried sausage, cheese, bread, fruit, clothing, writing kits. They even managed to smuggle in miniature Bibles and a few other books for the voyage, one of which would shape the course of Jacob's destiny.

The book in question was at first given to Professor Bourget by a rosy-faced Englishman with sparse white hair for whom Jacob acted as interpreter. Delpech still possessed remnants of English, having learnt it as a young man when his father had taken a position there in 1663 to learn about medicine. However, the book was of no use to the professor, a surgeon who knew only his mother tongue, German, Latin, and Greek. Jacob's father had been a physician and herbalist, and during previous conversations with Bourget, it had come to light that Delpech had always nurtured a fond interest in the Lord's natural world. So it was without regret that the professor gave the book to Jacob.

It was an old book that the elderly Englishman had kept since his younger days. He had spent half his career as a ship's surgeon for the East India Company. The book was *The Surgeon's Mate*.

*

On the twenty-first of November, one month to the day of her arrival, the pink lowered her sails and turned her prow towards the open sea.

Jacob Delpech was eager to reach the New World. Before setting out from the Bay of Cadiz, he had been able to converse in his broken English with a Dutchman by the name of Marcus Horst, who was familiar with the West Indies. 'There are a great many islands, large and small,' he had said. 'You must hold firm. It would not be so difficult to escape to an English settlement by cargo ship. From there you can gain passage aboard a ship bound for London or Amsterdam.'

La Marie and *La Concorde* were escorted by *Le Solide*, commanded by Admiral Chateaurenaud, chief of the French fleet. As they left the Bay of Cadiz, Jacob knelt with a group of fellow inmates to give thanks to God for the reprieve before the storm, and for the rays of light that had brought them comfort, hope, and their Holy Bibles.

The sound of the key in the lock made Jacob look up in time to see the door swing open. Next thing, he saw two men, two buckets, and a shaft of seawater.

'Enough of yer jabbering to false gods!' bellowed one of the guards.

'Or we'll come in and search yer all for fake Bibles,' said his mate. 'And if we find any, it's twelve lashes for heresy!'

Get VOYAGE OF MALICE today!
Available from Amazon and all major high street bookstores.

ABOUT THE AUTHOR

Paul C. R. Monk is the author of The Huguenot Connection historical fiction trilogy and the Marcel Dassaud books. You can connect with Paul on Facebook at www.facebook.com/paulcrmonkauthor and you can send him an email at paulmonk@bloomtree.net should the mood take you.

ALSO BY PAUL C.R. MONK

Have you read them?

In the *HUGUENOT CONNECTION* Trilogy

VOYAGE OF MALICE (Book 2)

Geneva, 1688. Jeanne dreams of her previous life as a wealthy merchant's wife before Louis XIV's soldiers ran her family out of France for refusing to renounce their faith. Jacob hopes his letters make it to Jeanne from the other side of the ocean. As he bides his time as an indentured servant on a Caribbean plantation, tragedy strikes in the form of shipwreck and pirates. If Jeanne and Jacob can't rise above a world that's closing all its doors, then they may never be reunited again…

LAND OF HOPE (Book 3)

A 17th Century family torn apart. A new power on the throne. Will one man reunite with his wife and child, or is he doomed to die in fresh battles? Land of Hope is the conclusion to the riveting Huguenot Connection historical fiction trilogy.

Also in the The Huguenot Connection series

MAY STUART

Port-de-Paix, 1691. May Stuart is ready to start a new life with her young daughter. No longer content with her role as an English spy and courtesan, she gains passage on a merchant vessel under a false identity. But her journey to collect her beloved child is thrown off course when ruthless corsairs raid their ship. Former French Lieutenant Didier Ducamp fears he's lost his moral compass. After the deaths of his wife and daughter, he sank to carrying out terrible deeds as a pirate. But when he spares a beautiful hostage from his bloody-minded fellow sailors, he never expected his noble act would become the catalyst for a rich new future.

Other works

STRANGE METAMORPHOSIS

When a boy faces a life-changing decision, a legendary tree sends him on a magical expedition. He soon has to vie with the bugs he once collected for sport! The journey is fraught with life-threatening dangers, and the more he finds out about himself, the more he undergoes a strange metamorphosis.

"A fable of love and life, of good and evil, of ambition and humility."

Winner of the LITERARY CLASSICS Eloquent Quill Youth Fiction Book Award.